ARIEL

By Alexande

Translation and cover art by Ma

by 123RF

Editing by PubRight Manuscript Services

CREATESPACE EDITION

*****

PUBLISHED BY:

TSK Group LLC for CreateSpace

ARIEL

Copyright © 2013 by TSK Group LLC

CreateSpace Edition License Notes

This book is licensed for your personal enjoyment only. If you would like to share this book with another person, please purchase an additional copy for each person you share it with. If you are reading this book and did not purchase it, or it was not purchased for your use only, then you should return to Amazon.com and purchase your own copy. Thank you for respecting the author's work.

TABLE OF CONTENTS

TABLE OF CONTENTS	2
CHAPTER ONE. THE CIRCLES OF HELL	1
CHAPTER TWO. DANDARHAT	13
CHAPTER THREE. MISTER HYDE'S EXPERIMENTS	21
CHAPTER FOUR. FRIENDS	36
CHAPTER FIVE. ON THE NEW PATH	40
CHAPTER SIX. TO THE UKNOWN DESTINY	49
CHAPTER SEVEN. BODEN AND HESLON	57
CHAPTER EIGHT. THE STUMBLING BLOCK	64
CHAPTER NINE. THE HUMAN ANT HILL	67
CHAPTER TEN. HOMELESS BEGGARS	72
CHAPTER ELEVEN. "LET'S BE HONEST – WE WERE BOTH WRONG."	80
CHAPTER TWELVE. AIRBORNE STOWAWAYS	85
CHAPTER THIRTEEN. VISHNU AND PARIAHS	89
CHAPTER FOURTEEN. EVEN GODS CAN BE JEALOUS OF PEOPLE	99
CHAPTER FIFTEEN. CAN DUST DREAM OF THE SUN?	104
CHAPTER SIXTEEN. TRAPPED AGAIN	109
CHAPTER SEVENTEEN. THE BONE OF CONTENTION	113
CHAPTER EIGHTEEN. UNSUCCESSFUL SEARCH	124
CHAPTER NINETEEN. THE MASTER IS DISPLEASED	128

CHAPTER TWENTY. PEACE IS RESTORED	134
CHAPTER TWENTY-ONE. AGREED	142
CHAPTER TWENTY-TWO. THE NEW TOY	148
CHAPTER TWENTY-THREE. MOHITA GATHERS DATA	152
CHAPTER TWENTY-FOUR. DOWN COMES THE STORM	161
CHAPTER TWENTY-FIVE. THE MASTER CHANGES HIS MIND	166
CHAPTER TWENTY-SIX. STRUGGLE FOR SURVIVAL	169
CHAPTER TWENTY-SEVEN. AN UNEXPECTED FIND	173
CHAPTER TWENTY-EIGHT. HE FLEW AWAY	175
CHAPTER TWENTY-NINE. THE AIR BATTLE	178
CHAPTER THIRTY. ALONE IN HEAVEN AND ON EARTH	181
CHAPTER THIRTY-ONE. IN THE JUNGLE	187
CHAPTER THIRTY-TWO. THE NEW CONVERT	194
CHAPTER THIRTY-THREE. "MIRACLE"	200
CHAPTER THIRTY-FOUR. OBSESSION	207
CHAPTER THIRTY-FIVE. TALKING BUSINESS	212
CHAPTER THIRTY-SIX. FLIGHT	215
CHAPTER THIRTY-SEVEN. HEAVENLY CONTRACTOR	218
CHAPTER THIRTY-EIGHT. "ALL THINGS PASS LIKE A DREAM"	225
CHAPTER THIRTY-NINE. "ELEVATED" CONVERSATION	231
CHAPTER FORTY. "BINOY THE UNDEFEATED"	235
CHAPTER FORTY-ONE. TWO WORLDS	239

CHAPTER FORTY-TWO. A SUFFERING MOTHER	**245**
CHAPTER FORTY-THREE. ANOTHER LIE	**251**
CHAPTER FORTY-FOUR. RETURN TO FRIENDS	**259**
ABOUT THE AUTHOR	**265**
ABOUT THE TRANSLATOR	**269**
END NOTES	**270**

CHAPTER ONE. THE CIRCLES OF HELL

Ariel sat on the floor near the low window of a room that resembled a monk's cell. The furniture comprised a chair, a stool, a bed and a woven mat in the corner.

The window looked out into the dull and quiet courtyard. There wasn't a single shrub or blade of grass. It was all sand and gravel, like a corner of the desert surrounded by four prison-like walls of a gloomy building with tiny windows. The palm tree tops from the luxuriant park surrounding the school barely rose above the flat roofs. A tall fence separated the park and the buildings from the outside world.

Deep silence was broken only by the crunching of the gravel under the unhurried feet of the school's teachers and overseers.

Other students brought to the Dandarhat school in Madras from all corners of the world occupied its bare cells that looked just like Ariel's. The age groups included everyone from eight-year old children to almost fully grown young men and women. They made up a kind of family, but their few quiet words and their eyes held neither love, nor friendship, nor attachment, nor joy when they met, nor grief when they were parted.

These emotions were eliminated by the teachers the moment a student arrived at the school, using all possible measures. The staff included Hindu Brahmins, hypnotists and European, predominantly English, occultists from the more recent movements.

Ariel wore a tunic – a long shirt with short sleeves made of coarse cloth. He was barefoot.

He was a tall, fair-haired youth of about eighteen. But one would have judged him younger by looking at his face: the pale-gray eyes gazed with childish naiveté, while his high forehead was already marked with light creases, like that of a man who had seen much and thought much. The color of his hair and eyes indicated European origins.

Ariel's face, with regular Anglo-Saxon features, was as motionless as a mask.

He gazed out the window vacantly, like someone deep in thought.

He was indeed pondering something: Ariel's tutor Charaka-*babu* ordered him to summarize his day every evening – remember all events that took place between sunrise and sunset, determine his own attitude toward these events, clarify his thoughts, desires and deeds. Before going to bed, Ariel was expected to give Charaka a full report, a kind of confession.

Setting sun lit the palm leaves and clouds flying swiftly across the sky. It had just stopped raining, and the warm moist air breezed into the cell from the courtyard.

What happened during the day?

Ariel woke up at dawn, as usual. He bathed, prayed, and had breakfast in the common dining area. The meal consisted of luchi – flatbread of plain flour and water, served on heavy wooden trays, as well as completely inedible fried peanuts and water in clay jugs.

Satia, the overseer, shifted his oppressive gaze from one student to the next and told them that they were eating bananas, tasty rice cakes with sugar and drinking whole milk. The students easily fell under the power of his suggestion and happily ate all the food. Only one boy, who was new and unprepared for the mass hypnosis, asked, "But where are the bananas? Where are the rice cakes?"

Satia walked up to the boy, tipped his head up by the chin and said imperiously, gazing into his eyes, "Sleep!" He then repeated the suggestion, after which the boy started hungrily consuming the coarse peanuts, mistaking them for bananas.

"Why are you wearing a scarf?" another overseer, a thin Indian man with a black beard and shaved head, asked a girl of about nine.

"I am cold," she replied, shrugging her thin shoulders. She was feverish.

"You are hot. Take off the scarf immediately!"

"Uhh, it's scorching hot!" the girl exclaimed, taking off her scarf and brushing her forehead with her arm, as if to wipe off the sweat.

Satia began reciting a sermon: all students must be insensitive to cold, heat, or pain. Spirit must rule over body!

The children sat quietly, their movements were listless and apathetic.

Suddenly, the same boy who asked about the bananas at the start of breakfast pulled a piece of flatbread from his neighbor, laughed loudly and stuffed it into his mouth.

Satia was next to the offender in one leap and pulled his ear. The boy started crying. All the children seemed to be dumbstruck by such unprecedented violation of discipline. Laughter and tears were ruthlessly eliminated at the school. Satia grabbed the boy with one hand and picked up a large jug with another. The boy went quiet, only his arms and legs shook.

Ariel felt sorry for the boy.

He lowered his head to keep from betraying his feelings. Yes, he felt very sorry for this eight-year old kid. But Ariel knew that by commiserating with another student he was committing a serious misdeed, in which he would have to confess to Charaka.

"Should I?" a thought flickered, but Ariel suppressed it. He was accustomed to great care in concealing his thoughts.

Following Satia's orders, a servant took away the small boy, forcing him to carry the large jug on his head. The breakfast was finished in complete silence.

Several young men and women who graduated were expected to leave the school that morning after breakfast.

Ariel felt hidden sympathy toward two of them – a dark-skinned wide-eyed boy and a slender girl. He had reasons to believe that they too considered him a friend. They were tied together by the several years spent in Dandarhat. They were forced to conceal their feelings under the mask of coldness and indifference. In those rare moments when they weren't watched by the overseers and tutors, the secret friends exchanged eloquent gazes or rare handshakes, but that was all. All three kept their friendship secret, for it was the only treasure that warmed their young hearts, like a small flower that miraculously managed to survive in the middle of a desert.

Oh, if their instructors knew of their secret! With what savage cruelty they would have crushed that flower! They would have forced the three friends to confess everything under hypnosis and then killed that warm feeling, replacing it by true coldness and true indifference.

They said their good byes in the courtyard near the iron gates. The graduates said in an icy tone, without raising their eyes, "Farewell, Ariel!"

"Farewell, farewell," and they parted, unable to even shake hands.

Keeping his head low, Ariel went back to the school, trying not to think of his friends and suppressing the feeling of sadness. There would be time for secret thoughts and feelings late at night. He would not confess them to anyone, even under hypnosis. That was Ariel's last and deepest secret, of which neither the cunning Charaka nor the school's Headmaster Bharava suspected.

Classes followed – history of religion, occultism, and theosophy. Dinner with "bananas", English, Hindustani, Bengali, Marathi, Sanskrit… A meager supper…

"You have eaten your fill!" Satia told them.

The supper was followed by a "séance". Ariel has already been through this terrible circle of the Dandarhat hell, but he had to be present during the "practical lessons" with the new students.

A dark narrow corridor lit only by a weak, flickering lantern with a smoking wick made of low-grade cotton, led into a large windowless room with another similarly dull light. There was no furniture in the room, save for a coarse table and several straw mats on the floor.

Ariel stood silent and motionless in the corner, along with a group of other senior students.

A servant led in a fourteen-year old boy.

"Drink!" a tutor said, holding out a mug.

The boy obediently swallowed the pungent-smelling and somewhat bitter liquid, trying not to wince. The servant quickly took off the boy's tunic and anointed his entire body with quickly evaporating ointments. The boy became consumed by anxiety and deathly longing. These feelings were followed by excitement. He began breathing heavily, his pupils widened, and his arms and legs twitched, like a marionette's.

The tutor held up the lantern with its flickering flame and asked, "What do you see?"

"I see the dazzling sun," the boy replied, squinting.

All his senses were elevated. A loud whisper sounded like thunder, he could hear spiders crawling up and down the wall, the breathing and heartbeat of every person in the room, the rustling of bats somewhere in the attic. He could see, hear, notice, and sense things that no normal person would be aware of.

For some students, this state resulted in delirium, for others – in a severe nervous breakdown. Some were never seen again after these trials: they either died or went mad.

Ariel himself had a very strong constitution. He went through all the trials and managed to preserve his health and sanity.

Back in his room, Ariel watched the first stars, when the door opened. Charaka entered, leading a dark-skinned boy with a frightened face.

"Sit!" he ordered the boy.

The boy sat down like a puppet. Ariel approached Charaka and bowed.

"He is new. His name is Sharad. You shall lead him tonight. Are you pleased with yourself?"

"Yes, father," Ariel replied.

"You have nothing to confess?" Charaka asked doubtfully. "Perfection can only be reached by he who is never completely pleased with himself." Charaka gazed into Ariel's eyes inquisitively and asked, "Did you think about the past?"

"No," Ariel replied firmly.

The students were forbidden to think about their lives prior to coming to the school, to remember their early childhood and their parents, to ask questions regarding their past and future. None of the students knew what awaited them, what they were being prepared for, and almost none remembered their past. Those who still had fresh persistent memories were forced to forget under hypnosis.

Charaka peered at Ariel once again and left.

Sharad sat in the same pose, as motionless as a small bronze idol.

Ariel listened to Charaka's fading footsteps and smiled for the first time during the entire day.

The Dandarhat students had only two paths to choose from. For the majority there was the utter, absolute deprivation of free will and, in the best case, a completely unstable nervous system. For a tiny minority comprising the physically and mentally stronger people, there was a path of most sophisticated hypocrisy, of most cunning deceit and most skilled simulation. Ariel belonged to the latter group. He was one of the few who managed to resist hypnosis, artfully imitating the somnambulistic state. But those like him were few and far between. It took but the smallest error for the deception to be unveiled. The instructors were the masters of their students' bodies and souls.

Ariel approached Sharad quickly and silently and whispered, "They will try to scare you, but don't be afraid, no matter what you see. It's done on purpose..."

The boy looked at Ariel with surprise and mistrust. No one at the school ever spoke to him in a friendly way.

"The main thing is not to cry or scream, if you don't want to get a beating!"

Sharad stopped crying.

Bats dashed back and forth silently beyond the window, sometimes flying into the room. Small lizards hunted bugs on the walls. The boy started watching them and calmed down.

Ariel lit an oil lamp. The red flame cast weak light around the room. The wind caused the flame to flicker, making Ariel's shadow dance on the wall. The corners of the room remained dark.

Something moved in the corner across from the boy. Sharad peered and went cold with terror. A large yellow snake with a short fat head, bulging neck and a flat belly was crawling out of a crack. It had a pale pattern on its lower neck, outlined with black lines. The pattern looked like eyeglasses. A *naja*!

The first *naja* – or the spectacled cobra – was followed by the second dark-brown one, and then the third one – completely black, and a gray one and another, and another. The snakes spread through the room surrounding the boy.

"Sit and don't move. Be quiet," Ariel whispered, as emotionless as ever and seemingly frozen on the spot himself.

The snakes came closer and closer. They rose high on their tails, their necks widened like flat shields, they rocked and stared straight at the boy, ready to attack.

Ariel whistled a dull monotonous tune with only three notes.

The snakes halted, listened, then lowered their heads and slowly crawled back into the corner, disappearing through an opening in the floor.

Sharad continued to sit motionless. Drops of cold sweat trickled down his face.

"Well done," Ariel whispered. But the praise was undeserved: the reason the boy did not scream or move was that he was paralyzed with fear.

A gust of wind burst into the room, bringing with it the sweet scent of jasmine.

Clouds obscured the stars. There was a clap of thunder, soon followed by the drumming of a tropical downpour. The air grew cooler. Lightning flashed, turning the building across white for a moment and reflecting in the water that quickly covered the courtyard, turning it into a lake.

The boy sighed in relief and shifted. However, his trials weren't over yet.

A woven screen separating two rooms suddenly rose and Sharad saw a brightly lit room with its floor covered with white plastic. An enormous tiger stood in the middle of the room. Light hit it in the eyes, and the golden striped beast squinted and shook its head in displeasure. Its thick tail flicked across the floor.

Finally, the tiger's eyes became used to the light. It narrowed its eyes at Sharad, growled briefly, then settled onto its haunches, preparing for a jump.

Sharad wrapped his arms against his head and screamed desperately.

He felt that someone was touching his shoulder. "It will rip me apart!" the boy thought, cold with terror. But the touch was too light for a large beast.

"Why did you scream?" he heard Ariel's voice. "The overseer will punish you for it! Come!" Ariel took Sharad's hand and forced him to stand.

Only then did Sharad dare open his eyes. The woven screen was back in place. The room was dark. The rain shower was fading away beyond the window, while thunder still rumbled in the distance.

Sharad stumbled after Ariel, barely aware of what was going on.

They passed through a long dark corridor and entered a narrow door. Ariel let Sharad go in first and said loudly, "Go! There is a staircase. Watch your feet." He added in a whisper, "Be careful. Do not scream, no matter what happens. Do not be afraid. They are trying to scare you to teach you to not be scared of anything."

Ariel remembered the first time he had to go through these trials. He had to walk alone with no one to warn or console him.

Sharad shakily descended the crumbling steps. A dark basement was before him. It smelled dank. The air was still and heavy. The stone floor was covered with cold slimy mud. Large drops of moisture fell from above. Water bubbled somewhere. The boy, not knowing which way to go, reached out to keep from hitting some invisible obstacle.

"Keep going, keep going," Ariel nudged him.

Sharad moved forward in the darkness. Muffled moans, wild howls, and insane laughter sounded from somewhere. They were followed by sinister silence. But the darkness felt as if it was filled with living creatures. Sharad could feel someone's cold touch. Suddenly, there was a monstrous laugh that caused the ground to shake.

"Keep walking!"

The boy touched a slimy wall on one side. Soon, his other hand brushed against the opposite wall. The dungeon seemed to grow narrower. Sharad was having difficulty moving forward.

"Keep going!" Ariel ordered. Then he whispered, "Don't be afraid, a little longer…"

But he didn't finish. Sharad felt the ground slipping away from under his feet and fell.

He landed onto something soft and damp. A heavy ceiling bore down on him and pressed him to the ground. He felt as if he was about to suffocate and moaned.

"Quiet," Ariel's whisper sounded.

The ceiling rose. The same darkness was all around. Suddenly, a white cloud emerged from the darkness. It took on a shape of a giant old man with a long white beard. His bony hand rose from the folds of his fog-like glowing robe. A dull low voice sounded.

"If you want to live, rise and walk. Do not look back."

Sharad obeyed. Crying quietly, he rose and walked down another corridor. The walls of the dungeon started glowing dull red. The air turned warm at first and then intolerably hot. The walls grew redder and started moving closer. Flames burst through the cracks and turned brighter and nearer with each step. A moment longer and Sharad's hair and clothes would catch fire. He gasped and felt faint. Someone caught him and the last thing he heard was Ariel's whisper, "Poor Sharad…"

CHAPTER TWO. DANDARHAT

Ariel woke up and his first thought was, "Poor Sharad!"

Sharad's nervous shock was so great that he had to be taken to the school's infirmary. The doctor made Sharad drink some hot milk with vodka, and the child fell asleep, while Ariel, his unwilling guide, returned to his room.

While Ariel bathed, the sun rose. The school gong rang. Instead of the coarse everyday tunic, Ariel put on a linen robe. The school was expecting important visitors.

After breakfast, the instructors and senior overseers gathered in a large hall with rows of armchairs, plain chairs and benches. At the far end of the long hall there was a carpet-covered stage decorated with garlands of flowers. The windows were shut and the hall was lit by electric lamps mounted in fanciful bronze chandeliers.

Soon the guests began arriving dressed in a variety of styles. There were imposing swarthy gray-bearded old men in silk robes decorated with pearls and jewels, emaciated fakirs, and representatives of various castes with their caste signs painted on their forehead with clay from the Ganges. The latter were dressed in coarse *dhoti*[i], the old-fashioned short jackets decorated with ribbons and handmade shoes with pointy tips. Some carried small copper pots on their sashes, after the ascetic fashion. There were others, dressed in nothing more than white sheets and wooden sandals.

The sahibs were the last to show up. The pale-skinned, tall, self-assured Englishmen in white suits took the front row armchair seats.

The school administration served them slavishly.

A pale-skinned man in an Indian costume came on stage. This was the school's headmaster Bharava. He greeted the guests in perfect, most sophisticated society English and asked them to "honor us by taking time to survey Dandarhat's achievements in our mission of upbringing the servants of peace, God and truth."

The instructors then demonstrated their most talented students. The entire event resembled the séances of "professors of magic and occult sciences" so popular in Europe.

The students paraded across the stage one after the other. They recreated entire scenes from books and plays, made speeches under hypnosis and repeated things mentioned by one of the guests with uncommon precision. Some of the students had such acute powers of observation that they noticed the movements of the guests that the others missed. According to some of the teachers, some students could see radiation emanating from the head of a person deep in thought and "hear the reflexive movement of the sound organs, involuntarily producing sounds to capture the thinking process". The implication was that the children could not only "see" but also "hear" the workings of one's brain. This was all demonstrated on stage, much to the approval of the guests.

Another group of youths were referred to as phenomena. They were allegedly capable of accumulating electrical charge sufficient to turn on a light bulb and produce sparks that surrounded their bodies like a halo. Yet others could see in the dark.

This group was followed by the specialists of a different kind. By listening to a few words from another person and observing his or her face, movements and other outward signs, they accurately summarized the most recent events from one's life.

Ariel watched this spectacle and thought, "They should demonstrate the trials the students have to go through instead."

Ariel has been through all the circles of hell. His last trial was "acceptance of the spirit". Ariel still shuddered when he remembered that dark ritual carried out by the students during the advanced stages of their education. They were forced to witness another man's death, hold his hands, and kiss him on the lips at the moment of death, taking in his last breath. It was a revolting ritual, but Ariel learned to restrain himself.

A noise distracted Ariel from his thoughts.

The headmaster invited the guests to another hall where they were to be treated to a different kind of performance.

The event that followed included awarding of diplomas to the members of the theosophical "White Council" by the "teacher of teachers" himself, known as Jesus Matreya.

The enormous hall was covered with greenery and flowers. The stage resembled a gazebo, with its carpets, ivy, roses and jasmine. Gusts of hot wind blew in through the window. The hall was becoming stuffy. Some of the visitors took off their shawls and fanned themselves with palm leaves. A fat *zamindar*[ii] surreptitiously stuffed a betel leaf into his mouth.

The front row included two gilded armchairs upholstered with yellow silk. They were occupied by an elderly Englishman in glasses, with a wavy gray beard, and by Madam-sahib – a plump woman with a fresh round face and short, curled, gray hair, who was dressed in an Indian costume. They were the leaders of the theosophical society – Mister Brownlow and Missus Dryden. The headmaster presented a bouquet of flowers to the lady.

When everyone took their seats, a choir of boys and girls in blue robes decorated with garlands of white oleanders, sang a hymn. Matreya appeared just as the last chords faded away.

Everyone rose. Some of the guests proceeded to fall to their knees.

The "teacher of teachers" was dressed in a long sky-blue robe. His head with wavy shoulder-length hair and a small beard resembled portraits of Christ by Italian artists. His handsome, effeminate face that some considered "blissful" was frozen in a grimace of "divine" smile. He lifted his arms in benediction.

Madam-sahib gazed at his striking face with delight. She admired him without any pretense of religious zeal.

The bearded Brownlow caught her gaze and frowned.

The award ceremony began, accompanied by many bows.

Some members of the council took off their medals and orders to receive them from Matreya's hands one more time and fell to the floor before him, while he lifted his arms above them and handed out flowers.

Then the "teacher of teachers" gave a speech and whipped the audience into such an exalted state, that there were hysterical screams, while some fainted or had seizures.

Having blessed everyone one more time, Matreya – the new embodiment of Buddha – left.

The sahib rose, offered Madam-sahib his arm. They walked through a door behind the stage with the air of people who knew their way around very well, and found themselves in a comfortable office, furnished after the European fashion including a fireplace, which was completely redundant in this heat.

The sahib sat down at the headmaster's desk and Madam-sahib took an armchair next to him.

The headmaster joined them shortly but did not sit down until his important guest said, "Have a seat, Mister Piers, and tell us how things are going."

Mister Piers, known as Bharava to the school's staff and students, ask Missus Dryden's permission to smoke a cigar and thought, "You know the answer to that better than I do."

That much was true.

Mister Piers and Mister Brownlow were both English and both worked in the same field. Religion – one of the fundamentals of the society they served – had sinister cracks in it and was losing its enchantment before the masses. They needed some kind of support and a range of surrogates or "replacements". They had to sustain the faith in the divine power and spirit, and strengthen people's mystical inclinations. That was where the theosophical, spiritual and occult societies came into play, performing and publishing thousands of books in all countries of the world. Their center was located in London. But India could not be ignored, for in the eyes of Europeans and Americans it was surrounded by the aura of mystery with its "occult knowledge", yogi and fakirs. In addition, religion in India was very helpful in sustaining the colonial influence of the English.

They built a splendid temple with a large dome. They also created the Dandarhat school near Madras to increase the numbers of adepts and priests of mysterious sciences, where the future "teachers of teachers" like Jesus Matreya – Krichnamutri Alcion – "the great teacher, akin to Krishna or Buddha" – were being prepared for their missions in Asia and Africa. The school also yielded a steady supply of mediums, prophets, hypnotists, mages and mind-readers for the fashionable European and American salons.

The Madras school was not an official establishment. The reasons for such arrangement were not just the unusual routines and methods of upbringing, but also the more practical considerations. Parents, relatives and guardians placed children there for the purpose of getting rid of them once and for all. Some children had been kidnapped by the Dandarhat agents.

The students were taught only the religious history and language of the countries where they were expected to eventually serve.

The most gifted or, rather, the most emotionally unstable of the graduates remained at the school to serve as overseers.

Hypnosis played a huge role in the school's system. The extreme enhancement of some students' perception made it possible to parade them as "mind readers" who perceived the subtle movements of lips and eyes and small sounds made by their instructors.

There were those capable of other "miracles". The tricks with glowing auras around the children's bodies, or delicate floral fragrances emitted by the "saints" were cleverly conceived and carried out, serving the same purposes. The overseers and "scientific consultants" of the school included many talented and knowledgeable people.

Such was the Dandarhat school.

Mister Piers puffed on his cigar and made his report. Brownlow and Dryden nodded their approval.

"What is the status of the graduates?" Mister Brownlow asked.

Piers named several students, explained their specialties and places they were destined for.

"I haven't decided what to do with Ariel yet," Piers said.

"Is that the difficult one?" Brownlow asked. "What is his real name?"

"Aurelius Galton."

"Right. Was he placed here by his guardians?"

"Exactly right," Piers replied. "Mister Boden and Mister Heslon from London. They have inquired about him recently. I replied that Aurelius' health was excellent, but…"

Brownlow winced involuntarily, made an impatient gesture with his fingers, cast a furtive glance at Missus Dryden, who was not supposed to know everything, and interrupted Piers, "Then what do you wish to do with him?"

"I can only tell you that he is not suitable for a medium, a mind reader, or a prophet. Ariel's head is too strong for that as is his overly healthy nervous system," he added with a hint of disappointment and even guilt. "He is difficult. Besides, these Boden and Heslon…"

"I know. They wrote to me as well," Brownlow interrupted once again. "Charles Hyde has some interesting news. Talk to him about Ariel. Perhaps he will be a good match."

"Who is this Charles Hyde?" Missus Dryden asked.

"You don't know him?" Piers addressed her courteously. "He is one of the scientific consultants of our school. A very interesting man."

"Talk to him then!" Brownlow repeated, rising.

CHAPTER THREE. MISTER HYDE'S EXPERIMENTS

"A man-fly you say? Ha-ha-ha! Until now people only knew how to make an elephant out of a fly, but you want to make a fly into a man."

"I do not want to make a fly into a man."

"Right, you want to make a man into a fly. Even better. Ha-ha-ha!"

This conversation took place in the laboratory of Charles Hyde, a great scientist who did not receive recognition elsewhere and found a home at Dandarhat. The place suited him. His competitors long since stated that Hyde belonged in a madhouse. The only difference between a mental institution and Dandarhat was that the former existed for treating and helping the patients, while Dandarhat turned healthy people into the mentally ill.

There were mentally unstable people among the overseers and "scientific consultants", although some of them were remarkable people in their own way. Hyde was one of them.

The open windows of a narrow, hallway-like laboratory were covered with woven curtains to protect against the light and scorching rays of the sun. Tables crowded with strange devices of all shapes and sizes loomed in the twilight. Cubes, globes, cylinders, and disks made of copper, glass and rubber were entangled in wires that looked like vines. It was a real jungle of scientific equipment, not easily penetrable for the uninitiated. There were no books, however. The entire colossal library dedicated to a variety of sciences was located within Mister Hyde's enormous, completely bald hydrocephalic skull, as red as a ripe tomato. The owner of remarkable memory, he could extract any reference from his brain at any time.

During the years spent in India, Hyde became fat and lazy, grew out a thick red beard and adopted local habits.

He lay sprawled on the mats for hours, dressed only in a pair of short white pants. Next to him was a jug with ice and lemons, a tin with betel and another tin with tobacco. His lips seemed covered in blood from the betel-colored saliva. In one hand he had a fan, with which he fanned himself constantly, in the other – a smoking pipe. He chewed betel, smoked, and pondered, from time to time asking his two assistants – a Bengal and an Englishman – to write down thoughts that occurred to him or to conduct an experiment. If they made mistakes, Hyde became irritated and yelled at them, but never got up. A minute later he laughed merrily.

At his feet, on a low bamboo stool, sat his Dandarhat colleague, another underappreciated scientist, Oscar Fox. He was ascetically thin, and his clean-shaven face was yellow from malaria. This glum hollow-cheeked face bore the air of an embittered loser. He spoke in a tone of an undeservedly offended man, never took his eyes off his wrist watch, and punctually opened a tin pillbox every fifteen minutes to swallow another pill.

Hyde and Fox have been working on one of Dandarhat's more complex challenges for over a year – a problem of creating a flying man, of finding a way to enable a person to fly without any device, the way people flew in their dreams. If the discovery was kept secret, theosophists and occultists would obtain a new powerful weapon for propagating their ideas. Many wonderful performances could be staged with a flying man, leaving contemporary scientists dumbstruck. Such a task was most suitable for the scientists like Hyde and Fox, who had a bit of adventuresome charlatanism in them and a bit of a dream, but were unquestionably talented. At Dandarhat they found what they could not have found elsewhere: financial support for realizing the most fantastic projects. They invented many "miracles of black and white magic" for Dandarhat. But all of them were no more than clever tricks. The matter of a flying man was more complicated.

Hyde and Fox approached the problem by following different paths. Fox was an engineer and a physicist, whereas Hyde was a biophysicist. Fox was the type of scientist who applied enormous effort to his work but constantly doubted the possibility of success. He never attacked a scientific problem head-on, he conducted numerous preliminary experiments, he beat around the bush, starting things and abandoning them. Not trusting himself, he often talked to Hyde. The moment his colleague expressed doubt or made fun of him, Fox abandoned his project and thought up a new one.

Hyde, on the contrary, was self-assured and ploughed on relentlessly. Hyde never told Fox how he was planning to create a flying man. The only thing he disclosed was that "the solution shall be based on physics, physiology, and biophysics."

This time the conversation began with Fox's statement, "I think I have stumbled upon a promising idea. The solution to the problem of a flying man is within the flight mechanics of a fly."

When Hyde stopped laughing, Fox started explaining indignantly, that the idea was nearly as funny or ridiculous as his esteemed colleague implied.

He spoke at length about the observations the other scientists made of the flight mechanics of a fly, and how complex that seeming simplicity was. He spoke about special muscles in a fly's chest – the muscles of "direct" and "indirect" influence. The fly's wingtips outlined a figure eight. Thanks to this peculiar movement, a fly could move with relatively little energy loss and a comparatively small wing area to elevate the substantial weight of its body. If they were to create an apparatus based on these principles, a man could fly with the aid of small wings, without any motors, using solely his own musculature.

"Splendid! Charming! Delightful! Enchanting! Wonderful!" after every word, Hyde laughed and fanned his face.

Fox turned yellow with indignation and asked, "What is so funny about this? Either you did not understand me or..."

"Or you are the one who did not understand anything," Hyde interrupted. "Yes, clearly you did not comprehend the essence of this task. What do you suggest? A new flying machine. Nothing more. A machine. A mechanism that can be hoisted onto the shoulders of any idiot..."

"Why an idiot?"

"A machine that can be launched into mass production and create hundreds, thousands of flying people. With a project like that you shouldn't be at Dandarhat, you should be working for the Ministry of Defense. Flying soldiers, scouts, snipers, bombers – that is all fine and good, of course. In general, this is not a bad idea. We could do away with stairs, elevators, escalators! Flying people could emerge from the windows of their skyscrapers like bees from a hive and fly down the streets. Wonderful! And what an opportunity for the mountain climbers! With their fly wings, they will cover Everest and Mont Blanc like real flies would converge upon a lump of sugar. You see, you even managed to get me excited about your project. But, my dear man, what we need is completely different! We must create a phenomenon – a man who can fly without any device. Who can just decide to fly – and fly."

"But if such a man can be created, than he too can be replicated by hundreds and thousands, can he not?"

"Of course he can."

"Then what's the difference?"

"The difference is that one would only need to capture your flying man, and any engineer, having examined your apparatus, could make another one like it. But if someone catches my flying man, he could discover or understand nothing. The secret is known only to me. And my flying man will be the only one in the world. Only I will be able to create the second one, or ten more – an only on Dandarhat's special orders. Do you understand?"

Fox was completely defeated. He swallowed a pill and it tasted particularly bitter. After a pause he said, "I consider what you are talking about simply impossible. It reminds me of the idle gossip about the levitation of the fakirs. Much has been said and written about it. But we scientists would do well to ignore these fairy tales. I have been living in India for nine years and have yet to see an example of levitation. If an eyewitness, a man I trusted, told me about it, I would have said to him, 'My friend you are a victim of clever deceit or hypnosis.'"

"Let's leave the fakirs to themselves. William!" Hyde shouted. A young man with a pale tired face came in from the next room. "Show Mister Fox experiment number one."

William left and returned bearing a tray with a small box.

"Unlock the box, Mister Fox, and raise the lid."

Fox turned the key cautiously. But he did not even have to open the box – the lid popped open on its own; a black porous mass the size of a fist suddenly flew out of the box, rose up vertically, hit the ceiling with a slight thud and seemingly stuck to it.

A puzzled Fox stared up at the sponge-like mass silently.

"Get it down, William!" Hyde ordered.

William brought in a ladder and climbed up to grab the sponge off the ceiling.

"Take it, Mister Fox, but hold tight, don't let it go."

Fox did not feel the sponge's weight. On the contrary, the porous mass seemed to exert a small, but palpable upward pressure. William took the sponge from Fox, put it back into the box, locked it up, and left.

"In this first experiment, I trespassed upon your area, Fox," Hyde said. "The physics of thin membranes. The porous mass has microscopically thin partitions in it, with the empty spaces filled with hydrogen. The first flying metal. Super-light, weightless, and finally flying materials! What a revolution in the construction and transportation industries! Skyscrapers reaching into the stratosphere, flying cities! I could have been swimming in gold for this invention. But they rejected me and did not appreciate me – all the worse for them! Let Dandarhat use my invention for its miracles! Imagine a boulder chained to the ground. A man walks up and pushes the boulder, the chains fall away and the man not only lifts the boulder, but flies into the air with it. Won't that be spectacular?"

"Do you call this levitation?" Fox asked mockingly. "Then a child's balloon is levitation as well!"

"I do not call this levitation," Hyde objected. "This would have been levitation had it been possible to create a man out of the porous weightless mass. Then a subtle tap with one foot would have been sufficient for that man to fly into the air. But such task is too much even for me. There is a simpler way. William! Show us experiment number two!"

William, as if waiting on them at a restaurant, brought out another wooden tray with a black box equipped with handles and a white cube on top of the box. William placed the tray on the floor in front of Fox.

"Turn the handle!" Hyde commanded.

Fax watched as the cube smoothly rose to the ceiling, hung there for a few moments and came down just as smoothly when William turned the handle back.

"Miracle of electrical engineering? Electromagnetism?" Fox asked.

"You are half correct!" Hyde replied with a laugh. "You are a physicist, figure it out!"

Fox stared at the cube dumbly. Hyde laughed again and said with satisfaction, "Yes, this nut would be tough to crack for modern physicists! My work is so far ahead that I can disclose a few things to you. Brownian molecular motion. Understand?"

Fox stared at Hyde silently, his eyes open wide.

"Surprised? Of course you are! Brownian motion is disorderly, chaotic. Probability theory tells us that theoretically it is possible for all molecules to head in the same direction at some point. And then a stone or a person could rise into the air. But the likelihood of such an occurrence equals a fraction of a percentage point with so many zeroes, that it is less possible in practice than the collision of the sun with some other celestial body. Putting it simply, it is almost zero. Normally, a particle hits other particles, experiences equal gravitational pull to move to the right, to the left, up and down and, therefore, remains in place. No wonder that modern scientists had stated, 'We cannot indulge in any illusions regarding the possibility of practical use of Brownian motion, for example, with the purpose of elevating bricks to the top of a building being constructed.' Thus, they have also given up on the possibility of a human body overcoming Earth's gravity. The entire question has been dismissed. But I thought: the idea of controlling the disastrous, destructive, untamable, willful power of lightning would have seemed equally mad and impossible to our ancestors from a few centuries ago. And yet, the same power currently flows through our wires, obligingly moving our machines and providing light and heat."

"So, you decided to control Brownian motion, the chaotic motion of molecules?"

"I didn't just decide it, as you can see, I have done it. William! Show Mister Fox the dance of the beakers!"

A long flat apparatus appeared on the table with glass beakers on top of it. The beakers suddenly started jumping higher and higher. Some of them moved up and down slowly, others dashed back and forth at great speed.

William turned a lever, and one of the beakers suddenly flew out the window.

"You see one of the stages of my work. This beaker quadrille had caused me a lot of trouble. It is easier to tame a hippo, an elephant, or a fly than a molecule. The main difficulty is that my molecular ballerinas move at very different speeds. The beakers contain molecules of hydrogen, nitrogen and carbon monoxide. Think about it, it's not easy to make the beakers dance at the same pace: at thirty-two degrees Fahrenheit the speed of hydrogen molecules equals five thousand five hundred and fifty-one feet per second, of nitrogen – one thousand four hundred eighty-nine, and carbon monoxide – even lower than that, at one thousand one hundred and eighty-seven feet per second. The speed of a hydrogen molecule surpasses not only that of a gun bullet, but also that of a cannonball, approaching the speed of the long-distance missiles. When temperature increases, so does the speed of the molecule's movement. Did you see that hydrogen beaker bolt out of here? Imagine bullets and missiles propelled by the inner forces of the molecules themselves!"

"How did you manage to turn the chaotic molecular movement into unidirectional?" Fox asked.

"It's a long story. Suffice it to say that, when studying the molecular movement, physicists only took into account the role of the temperature, ignoring electrical phenomena. I had to delve deep into the study of the complex game between forces that takes place within the atoms, of which molecules consist, and of the way of controlling this game."

"Then, essentially, it is no longer Brownian motion, but rather electrical," Fox said.

"The two are connected."

Fox thought about it.

"Suppose," he said, "you managed to control the molecular movement, engaging the factors of electric attraction and repulsion, changing of the potential, and recharging, if I understand you correctly. But everything you have shown me has been inorganic."

"Doesn't human body consist of inorganic elements, of molecules and atoms?" Hyde objected. "That is not the difficulty. The first problem is to bring the molecules naturally moving at different speeds to one common denominator, otherwise a human body would be simply pulled apart. I had to tie together two fields: physics and electrophysiology. To strengthen electric potential, I introduced various radioactive elements which provided the necessary radiation. I created a chain: from the brain impulse, a thought, to the nervous system; from the nervous system – to the electrophysical events and from there – to molecular control."

"Did you succeed?"

"Judge for yourself. Satish, bring the caterpillar!"

Hyde's second assistant brought a potted flowering plant with a caterpillar on one of the branches and struck the branch. The caterpillar fell off but stopped in the air halfway between the branch and the floor.

Fox moved his hand to check whether the caterpillar was hanging on a web string, but there was no web. Satish carefully took the caterpillar, put it back on the branch and took it away. After that, without waiting for another instruction, he brought in a small baby chick with half-grown wings and placed it on the floor.

Satish loudly clapped his hands. The frightened wingless chick suddenly rose into the air, fluttered about the room squeaking and flew out of the window into the park. Fox walked up to the window and watched the chick land in the grass.

"Stay at the window, Fox," Hyde said.

Satish walked out into the garden with a cat, placed it on a tree and called, "Kuday! Kuday! Come here! Look, there is a cat! A cat!"

There was barking and a little dog Kuday ran up to the tree.

Seeing the cat, the dog barked again, jumped and suddenly rose into the sky with a pitiful yelp. Its barking and squealing rapidly faded into the distance.

"Kuday! Kuday! Kuday!" Satish called.

The dog, having already reached the altitude of three hundred feet, started descending. Soon, it was back with Satish. It jumped happily and almost flew away again, but Satish caught it and took it away.

"The one before the last number on our program," Hyde said merrily. "Stay at the window, Mister Fox."

Satish placed a large toad onto the garden path and lightly nudged it with his foot. The toad jumped and flew over the shrubs and trees, higher and higher. Soon, it became lost in the distance, but Fox stared into the blue sky for some time after.

"Well, what do you think?" Hyde asked.

Fox sat down onto the chair, habitually glanced at his watch, gave a start, quickly swallowed two pills, but did not even feel their taste this time.

"I suppose we can safely call this levitation, can't we?" Hyde said, fanning himself. "If course, you have noticed the behavior of the subjects. The caterpillar has the ability to lower itself from a branch using a web string. I blocked its web-producing glands, so that it could not generate a string and hang on it. But the nervous centers continued working as usual and sending the corresponding impulses. That was enough to activate the reorganized molecular motion and produce the electric recharging of molecules with respect to Earth's electromagnetic field, causing the caterpillar to hang in the air.

"The baby chick is a bird that has almost forgotten how to fly, yet with the instincts required for flying are still in place. Using these instincts, it was able to use its new ability more fully than the caterpillar. The dog only knows how to jump. And even though it is a more intellectually developed animal, the sudden flight overwhelmed it, and it would have flown away and perished had Satish not called it back and given it a desire to return.

"As for the toad, which is at a fairly low stage of evolutionary development, it did perish, having reached the cold and oxygen-poor atmospheric layers. Experiments indicate that an animal's death eliminates its levitating ability, and our toad probably crashed onto the head of some stunned peasant. Although, the ability should really disappear at the end of life of the artificial radioactive elements. Complete control over levitation can only be achieved by a human being."

"You said that the experiment with the toad was the one before the last, but you have yet to show me the last one," Fox said.

"It's not difficult to guess that the last experiment will involve a human subject," Hyde replied.

"Will involve? Then you haven't performed the experiment yet?"

"You see, the foundation is in place," Hyde said. "Take the experiment with the dog, whose nervous system and both sides of the brain had no ill effects from levitation, despite the fact that large changes would take place in its organism, including blood circulation, nervous function and others. I am just waiting for..."

There was a knock on the door and Bharava-Piers entered.

"Ah, Mister Piers! Honorable guru! Bharava-*babu*," Hyde said mockingly. "What news?"

"Mister Brownlow sent me."

"Brownlow and I did have a talk. Whom did he choose?"

"Ariel. Aurelius Galton."

"Well then, Ariel shall be the first flying man," Hyde said indifferently.

"I see it as a sign of fate," Piers said, raising his eyes heavenward. "You know about the Dandarhat tradition to give the students new names. We named Aurelius Ariel because it sounded similar to his original name. But Ariel is also a satellite of planet Pluto. It also sounds similar to the word 'airy'. Uranus, god of heaven..."

"Mercy, Mister Piers! You have gotten so carried away by your role of Bharava *saniasi*[iii], that you forget who you are preaching to!"

"One's habit is second nature," Piers said with a smile and in a different tone of voice. "Here is what I wanted to ask you, Mister Hyde. Will the experiment endanger Ariel's life?"

"I don't think so," Hyde answered. "But if you value his life so highly, feel free to volunteer yourself. I don't care who to begin with. A flying headmaster! That would be sensational!"

Letting Hyde's joke slide, Piers asked another question, "Will the experiment put his mental faculties at risk?"

"Quite possibly."

"Not much we can do about that, can we? Considering the importance of our task, we are bound to take certain risks," Piers said with a sigh.

"I can't stand it when you speak with such a Jesuit air. I can see you through and through, Mister Piers. What you really want is for Ariel to remain alive, but go mad, but not so much that you couldn't use him for your theosophical and occult purposes. Ha-ha-ha! Isn't that so, you old fox?"

Piers was losing his temper but remembered Hyde's importance, controlled himself and replied dryly, "Our duty is to follow the divine path. I am very glad that you understand in which direction to apply your efforts. Ariel shall come to you this evening. But be careful, Mister Hyde. Prepare him for what he is about to become. A sudden ability to fly is nothing to joke about. We don't want him smashing his head."

CHAPTER FOUR. FRIENDS

Sharad came out of the infirmary and was assigned to Ariel's room. The relationship that became established between them was unusual for the Dandarhat students.

According to the school's rules, an older student was expected to guide his younger apprentice, becoming the first and closest overseer and "prophet", a guru. No closeness, affection, or friendship was allowed. Blind obedience of the younger student to the older was one of the foundations of the system. But Ariel managed to retain a deal of independence under the disguise of complete obedience. The sense of self-preservation forced him to be hypocritical and fake as much as he could. He became a true virtuoso. Ariel intended to lead Sharad down the same path. The kid instinctively figured out what was required of him. He learned to assume a devastated air when Ariel scolded him in front of others for things he did not do. When they were alone, however, Ariel whispered to his pupil the instructions that would have horrified Dandarhat's teachers and overseers. Sometimes Ariel blurted out, "I hate them so much!" and Sharad knew who he was talking about. Sharad hated Piers and all the other tormentors just as much, but in his case his emotions were curbed by fear. The boy shook and glanced around all the time, afraid for himself and for Ariel, when Ariel entrusted his most secret thoughts to him.

One evening, Ariel was talking quietly to Sharad. Bharava's creeping footsteps sounded from the corridor. Ariel, whose hearing was exceptionally good, immediately stepped away from the boy and started scolding him loudly. Sharad made a guilty face. Bharava entered the room, surveyed the students inquisitively, as usual, and addressed Ariel, "My son! We have brought you up and taken care of you to the best of our ability. It is time to reap the harvest. You are a young man. Your education is now complete. It is time to go to work and sever those who fed and educated you, thank them for their care, your room and board. Dandarhat bestowed a great honor upon you, designating you for great service, and I trust you will not disappoint us."

During that pompous speech, Ariel stared straight into Bharava's eyes, like a man who had nothing to hide. The youth realized that his fate has been decided and that his life was about to undergo a change. Not a single muscle twitched in his face and he showed no signs of anxiety.

Sharad also realized that he was about to be parted from the only person who made his existence easier. He wasn't yet capable of concealing his emotions like Ariel, and so he dropped his eyes and held his breath, because he didn't want to attract the attention of scary Bharava.

Ariel "took dust" from Bharava's feet, that is, leaned forward, touched Bharava's feet, then touched his forehead and said, "My thoughts, my desires, my deeds, and my life belong to you."

Bharava gave him another searching look and was pleased. For the first time in all the years of education he expressed affection – he touched Ariel's chin with his fingertips and then kissed them.

"Come with me, Ariel. Your step will be the first one on your new path!"

Ariel followed him like a well-trained dog.

Sharad was left alone, covered his face and, unable to hold back any longer, started crying.

He was overjoyed when at midnight, he suddenly felt a familiar hand on his shoulder and heard Ariel's whisper.

"Is that you, *dada*[iv]?"

"Yes, it's me, Sharad, don't be afraid."

"What happened to you, *dada*?"

"Quiet. Bharava… You know, he is not an Indian, but an Englishman. His name is Piers. He took me to Charles Hyde, the scientist. He is a sahib too. When Hyde saw Bharava, he exclaimed, 'Here you are, Mister Piers! And Ariel too?' Bharava got so angry and started winking at Hyde. Then Hyde corrected himself and said, 'Good evening, Bharava-baby!' But I already figured out that Bharava was not an Indian. Although, I suspected as much before. Everyone here lies every step of the way."

"So, what did he do, that Hyde guy?" Sharad asked impatiently.

"Hyde? He gave me a physical, like a doctor would, and then said to Bharava, 'He will do. He is completely healthy. In a few days we'll have him…' But then Piers started making faces at him again, and Hyde ordered me, 'Come early in the morning, before breakfast, understand? Before breakfast. Don't eat anything but clean yourself well. Take a bath, and not just the usual washing.' That's all."

"Then why were you gone so long?"

"Bharava instructed me, 'Obedience, obedience, obedience!'," Ariel laughed quietly.

That night, the friends slept little. Sharad grieved his upcoming separation from his friend. Ariel tried to guess what lay ahead.

CHAPTER FIVE. ON THE NEW PATH

After Ariel said good bye to Sharad the next morning, he went to see Hyde, who met him wearing a white doctor's coat and hat.

They entered a room that looked like a surgery combined with an x-ray laboratory, filled with unusual and complex equipment.

Hyde ordered Ariel to undress and lie down on a table covered with white plastic.

As usual, Ariel obeyed, assuming he was about to be hypnotized, which he knew how to skillfully fake. But he was mistaken.

Hyde ordered Ariel to swallow some powder dissolved in water and then shouted, "William, the mask!"

A young man in a white robe and hat pressed a mask over Ariel's face. The mask had a strong sickly smell.

"Breathe deeply, Ariel, and count loudly!" Hyde ordered.

"One...two...three..." Ariel began.

By the time he reached twenty he started becoming confused and, pausing, soon lost consciousness.

"It's all over," he heard when he came to and opened his eyes. He felt nauseous and his head was buzzing. He was no longer on the table, but on the floor in Hyde's study. "Do you feel bad? It's alright, it will pass. Just stay still for a bit," Hyde said.

The scientist was back on his woven mat, with his lips red from betel, smoking a pipe and fanning himself.

Remembering Piers' warning, Hyde decided to carefully prepare Ariel for the role of a flying man.

When Ariel fully recovered, Hyde asked, "Are you strong, Ariel? Could you lift a man your own size?"

"I have never tried, but I think I could," he replied after a pause. The Dandarhat life taught him to be careful in everything he said.

"Every healthy person can lift a weight equaling his own body and even more! William! Ride around on a chair!" the scientist ordered his assistant.

William, who already knew what was required of him, sat down on a chair backwards, wrapped his legs around the chair legs, and his arms – around the back, and started jumping, moving across the room in leaps, the way children would.

Ariel watched the galloping William in astonishment.

"Notice, Ariel, William's feet are not touching the floor. William is pulling the chair up and goes up with it. At each pull, he jumps up into the air by an inch or two and moves forward by just as much. Now, had William been stronger, wouldn't he jump higher and further? No? And the stronger he was, the further he would leap. There is nothing miraculous or unusual about it. So, here we are. Now listen closely, Ariel. While you were under anesthesia, while you slept I injected… introduced into your body a liquid that increases your power many times. And now you can ride a chair much better than William. Try it! Get up, take the chair and do as William did."

William surrendered his seat to Ariel, tied a rope to the chair's seat and held the end tightly.

"Jump, Ariel!"

Ariel pulled the chair and, quite unexpectedly to himself, made such a leap that he would have hit his head on the ceiling, had it not been for the rope. The rope also interrupted the arch-like pattern of his leap, and Ariel crashed to the floor along with the chair, and toppled William as well.

Hyde laughed loudly, and then frowned. He appeared suddenly anxious, so much so that he stopped chewing betel.

"Are you hurt, Ariel?"

"A little. Just my knee and elbow," Ariel replied, completely overwhelmed by what had happened.

"What did you feel when you flew?"

"I... It was as if something hit me lightly in the head and shoulders... Something was pressing me, but from the inside..."

"Right. Right. Just as I expected," Hyde mumbled. "But not too much, right? It didn't hurt?"

"No. Just in the first moment. I was very surprised and even a little frightened."

"Did it interfere with your thinking? Did you faint even for a second?"

"No," Ariel replied. "I don't think I did."

"Excellent!" Hyde exclaimed and mumbled, "At least, it's excellent for me. Piers won't be entirely pleased, but that's his problem. It's the rope's fault that you fell and hurt yourself. However, without it, you may have cracked your head against the ceiling. We used the rope because you don't know how to control your power yet. Listen, Ariel, listen carefully. You can now do what no other person can. You can fly. In order to fly, you only need to think about it. You can rise, fly faster or slower, turn in any direction, and descend as you wish. You just need to control yourself, the way you control your body when you walk, rise, sit or lie down. Understand? Well, try jumping on the chair again. Just don't pull the chair, but think that you need to go up and fly."

Ariel sat down, grabbed the chair's back and thought, "I shall rise!" He rose up three feet, circled the room and smoothly landed next to Hyde, still not quite believing what was happening.

"Well done! You are making quick progress."

"Can I fly without the chair?" Ariel asked.

Hyde laughed, spraying red saliva.

"Of course! Ha-ha-ha! Did you think that the chair was a flying machine, like a witch's broomstick? You are a flying man now. The first man to fly without any machines or wings. You should be proud!"

Ariel got off the chair. "Rise!" he thought and he rose and hung in the air.

"Ha-ha-ha! Swindler? Charlatan?" Hyde laughed, remembering his scientific colleagues who rejected him. "How about this?"

The door of the study opened. Bharava stood in the doorway, with Fox peeking over his shoulder.

Piers-Bharava, seeing Ariel between floor and ceiling, opened his mouth wide and seemed to freeze to the spot. Fox pursed his dry lips painfully and hunched into the shape of a question mark. Ariel turned smoothly, went down and up slowly.

"Come in, gentlemen! Don't be shy," Hyde invited them triumphantly.

Piers finally recovered and ran to close the window, grumbling, "So careless!" He then walked around Ariel, shaking his head.

"Congratulations, colleague!" Fox squeezed out, approaching Hyde and twisting his mouth into a smile.

"Well? Isn't this better than your fly?" Hyde asked, clapping Fox on the shoulder so hard that he staggered.

Ariel landed. Bharava-Piers ran to the phone, called Brownlow and asked him to come to Hyde's study immediately.

"How do you feel when you fly?" Bharava asked Ariel.

"Fine. At first it was a little unpleasant... over my body, in my shoulders..."

"Right, right! Are you dizzy? Do you feel confused?"

"No."

"Ariel's mental faculties are unharmed, alas... Hm... Yes, yes!" Hyde said.

Piers gave him a meaningful look.

Soon Mister Brownlow and Missus Dryden joined them.

Ariel was told to fly to the ceiling, fly around the room standing and lying, "like a fish" as Missus Dryden said, roll over and do various tricks. Missus Dryden gasped with fear and delight every minute and exclaimed, "Lovely! Wonderful! Charming!"

Brownlow was rubbing his hands, looking very pleased, and encouraged Ariel to do more tricks in the air.

"You'll wear him out!" Hyde exclaimed good-naturedly and ordered Ariel to come down.

Everyone except Hyde sat down, and Bharava, addressing Ariel, made a speech, which was as pompous as ever and peppered with quotes and eastern metaphors.

He once again spoke of the high honor bestowed upon Ariel, who was now almost a son to Indra, the god of sky and air, and brother to Maruta, the god of wind. He also mentioned the great power Ariel now had and the great responsibility that came with it.

Bharava leveled his hypnotic gaze at Ariel and imposed on him the unquestioning absolute obedience, and threatened him with terrible punishments for the slightest disobedience.

"Even if you think of flying away, remember, you shall suffer such terrible, painful, despicable death that no man has ever experienced. No matter where you go, to the tall mountains, into the dark jungle, into the wild deserts or to the edge of the world, remember, we shall find you anywhere, because our power is boundless. And then..." Bharava started describing various forms of torture and suffering so colorfully that Missus Dryden shivered and gasped. "Also remember: you must not tell a single person that you can fly. Don't dare speak about it. And don't dare fly or rise even an inch above the floor without our orders. Do not fly even if you are alone in the room!"

Bharava made gestures which were supposed to strengthen the suggestion. He then said sternly in his usual voice, "You may go to your room now. Remember what I said."

Ariel bowed and went to the door, trying to walk normally and feeling afraid that he might fly up with each step. "I must walk, walk – not fly!" he kept telling himself.

When Ariel left, Piers followed him with his eyes through the open door. He then sighed with relief and said, as if replying to his own thoughts, "No, he will not fly away! We have stripped away his will, just as with other Dandarhat students."

"Still, it was careless to let Ariel go on his own," Brownlow noted.

"Are you going to keep him on a chain and let him go only so high like a balloon?" Hyde asked mockingly.

"We could have sent him with a chaperone, who could hold his hand," Brownlow objected, "and then lock him in a room with no windows."

"What if he flew away with the chaperon?" Hyde continued just as mockingly.

Missus Dryden shrieked in surprise and Brownlow's eyebrows crept up almost to his forehead.

"Is that possible?"

"Entirely," Hyde replied, "as long as the chaperone is not much heavier than Ariel himself."

"Another complication," Brownlow exclaimed.

"You should have thought about it earlier. I've done my job, and how you plan to guard and demonstrate your Indra is not my problem," Hyde said.

"Mister Brownlow," Piers interjected, "your concerns are completely baseless. Ariel has long since been tied down by a strong chain: not only has he lost his free will, he is in a state of constant hypnotic trance. I have imposed complete obedience under hypnosis to him so many times, that he now accepts all my orders as absolute and will not violate them even under penalty of death. He is more captive than if he wore shackles. I take all responsibility."

Brownlow said with a shrug, "Very well!"

Hyde brought up his reward and started haggling noisily with Piers. They argued for so long that Missus Dryden, concerned that she might get a migraine, rose to leave. Brownlow got up as well.

"We shall discuss this later!" Piers said to Hyde and went to see the guests out.

They stepped outside, Piers walking with Brownlow and Fox with Missus Dryden.

She started asking Fox, how "this magician Hyde" managed to create a flying man, and, without listening to his answers, continued interrupting him with new questions, "Can he make flying animals? A cat for example?"

"Yes, I've seen a flying dog and then a toad."

"Splendid! I shall ask Mister Hyde to teach my little kitty Queen how to fly. She shall chase the bats away from the porch in the evenings. I am terribly frightened of them and they ruin the best part of my day. After all, here in India, in Madras, one can only feel alive in the evenings. Yes, it would be delightful!"

As Missus Dryden was not only an occult leader but also a poetess, she raised her colorless eyes to the sky and started improvising,

> *The skies were filled with ghostly bats,*
> *Who sped away from flying cats.*

Piers and Brownlow were having an entirely different conversation.

Piers asked Brownlow whether they would create more flying people with Hyde's assistance or whether Ariel was to be the only one. In the latter case, to ensure that Hyde did not get hired away by their enemies, should they take measures accordingly.

"Should we kill Hyde?" was the real question, and Brownlow understood it without words and said, "For now, let us make certain he has no compunction to leave us. We are not going to make any other flying people. But something might happen to Ariel. We still need Hyde. Just make certain that Hyde remains isolated from the outside world. Understood?"

Piers nodded and replied, "It shall be done."

CHAPTER SIX. TO THE UKNOWN DESTINY

Having left Hyde, Ariel followed a garden path toward the dormitory. He stepped slowly, as if learning how to walk, and pressed down with his sandals so hard that the sand that covered the path crunched under his feet. He had no doubt that he was being watched.

Ariel was still under the influence from his flights around the room. He could fly! The thought filled him with joyous emotion, the reasons of which he was afraid to ponder out there, in the garden, in broad daylight, under Bharava's gaze which he could still feel. Ariel suppressed the thoughts that sounded in his soul like a triumphant song, "Freedom! Release!" and did not let them rise to the surface of his conscience. He could only enjoy the echo of that song.

Only after turning the corner did he allow himself to think cautiously, making certain the thought did not transition into deed, "If I wanted to, I could rise and fly away from this hateful school and these terrible people." He pressed his feet into the sand even harder and more thoroughly.

During all his years at the school, Ariel never abandoned the thought of getting out, finding out about his past and looking for his family.

Despite the bans and hypnotic suggestions, whenever he remained alone at night, he tried to restore in his mind the memories of his early childhood, before coming to Dandarhat. Sometimes he saw the pictures from the past, the snatches preserved by his memory in his dreams, and the dreams were often more vivid than the conscious memories.

He saw a different country with a lead-colored sky, streetlamps glowing dully through brownish-gray fog, enormous buildings damp from rain, and people who appeared suddenly and disappeared just as suddenly in the dusky veils of fog.

He remembered sitting in a car and watching that smoky, dank, vague world through a window.

He remembered a large room and an enormous fireplace with flaming logs. Ariel sat on the floor building a house from toy bricks. A blond girl sat on a silk cushion next to him and handed him the bricks. An old lady with a black lace cap on her gray-haired head sat in a soft armchair by the fireplace reading a book and glancing sternly at them over her glasses from time to time.

A man in a black suit entered the room. He had mean round eyes, like an owl's, and a revolting fake smile. Ariel remembered being afraid of that man and hating him. The man in black walked across the carpet, smiling wider and wider, with malice in his eyes. He crushed the toy house under his feet. Ariel started crying and…woke up.

The reality remained the same – with palm leaves fluttering against the deep blue sky, large stars, bats dashing about. Stuffiness, India, Dandarhat….

Sometimes Ariel saw himself in a small stuffy room that was rocking. There were enormous terrible green waves beyond a round window. Across from Ariel, the black man sat on a couch, even more terrifying than the waves, the same man who crushed the toy house in his dreams or in reality.

His memory preserved no other recollections from early childhood. The terrors of Dandarhat Ariel had to go through obscured the past. But it lived in Ariel's soul, like a handful of plants in a desert.

All he ever knew was loneliness, joyless childhood and youth. He had no family or friends. ...Except Sharad. Poor Sharad! He had only just stepped on the first step of the staircase of torture. If only he could save him from this hell!

"I can fly..." But Ariel pushed the thought away with an effort of will and pressed his feet firmly into the sand.

"Ariel, *dada*!" Sharad whispered happily at the sight of his friend, but quieted when he saw the stern expression on his face. This wasn't a good time for a discussion.

The gong sound called everyone to breakfast and the two friends went to the dining room, silently ignoring each other.

That day Sharad received several reprimands from instructors for being absent-minded. The day dragged on slowly.

Before sunset, Bharava stopped by Ariel's room and told Ariel to remember and get a new robe from the purser.

"I shall come for you tomorrow at five in the morning. Be ready. Take a bath and put on your new clothes."

Ariel bowed obediently.

"How is Sharad?" Bharava asked before he left.

"He is having trouble mastering concentration," Ariel replied.

"You should punish him more strictly," Bharava said and, flashing Sharad an angry look, left.

Before bed Ariel made Sharad read a few excerpts from the sacred books, *Shastri*. He was calm, stern and requested that Sharad read loudly and slowly.

However, Sharad didn't miss a few of Ariel's glances at the window, followed by a shadow of concern. The trees in the park rustled from the gusts of wind, promising rain not far behind. There were distant claps of thunder, but the sky was still bright with stars. Only when the pale foggy strip of the Milky Way started darkening from an approaching cloud, Ariel breathed a sigh of relief. Soon, the first large raindrops hit the ground. The gong rang melodiously in the darkness – the signal to go to sleep.

Sharad slammed the thick book shut, and Ariel blew out the lantern. They sat on the mat, shoulder to shoulder, in the darkness and silence.

Sharad heard Ariel rise and rose with him. Ariel hugged him and lifted him up.

"You are so light," Ariel whispered and laughed quietly at something. "Would you like me to lift you even higher, Sharad?"

Sharad felt Ariel lift him up almost to the ceiling, hold him there and then lower him down. Were Ariel's arms really that long?

"Lie down, Sharad," Ariel whispered.

They settled down on the mat, and Ariel whispered into the boy's ear, "Listen, Sharad. Hyde made me into a flying man. I can fly like a bird now."

"But where are your wings, *dada*?" Sharad asked, patting Ariel's shoulders.

"I can fly without wings. The way we fly in our dreams. They probably want to show me to other people, like a miracle. And I... I want to fly away from Dandarhat!"

"What will happen to me without you, *dada*?" Sharad cried.

"Quiet! Don't cry. I want to take you with me. You are light, and I think I can fly away with you."

"Take me with you! Take me away from here, *dada*! It's so bad, so scary here. I shall die without you," the boy whispered.

"I'll take you with me. Can you hear the rain? Good. No one shall see us in the dark. The window is open. Tssss! Someone is coming. Be quiet."

The door creaked.

"Ariel, are you asleep?" they heard Bharava's voice. "Ariel!"

"Mmm..." Ariel hummed and then, as if waking up, exclaimed, "Ah, it is you, Guru Bharava!"

"Why did you not close the window, Ariel? Look at all this water on the floor!" Bharava closed the window, drew the curtains and left without a single word.

Ariel knew: Bharava was watching him and did not trust him. He could open the window, but what if Bharava left guards under it? The moment he raised the curtain, someone might sound an alarm.

Sharad lay on the mat shaking, as if in a fever. The downpour drummed behind the window. Thunderclaps came closer and closer and grew louder and more frequent. Lightning bathed the room in blue light through the pale curtains. Ariel stood by the window and frowned. He then took a towel off a wooden peg in the wall and whispered to Sharad, "Follow me."

They opened the woven drape separating them from the next room, walked through and then stepped into the corridor. It was completely dark. Ariel walked ahead, leading Sharad who was holding on to the end of the towel. Everyone was asleep. All was quiet. They went up and down stairways, passed quietly through long hallways and finally reached a steep wooden ladder.

Ariel pushed the trapdoor leading to the roof. They were instantly blinded by lighting, deafened by thunder, and soaked by rain. They walked up to the flat roof.

"Get onto my back, Sharad!" Ariel said.

Sharad climbed onto his back, Ariel tied him down with the towel, straightened out and looked around. At the flash of lightning, he saw the wide courtyard covered with water, like a lake, and the glistening buildings of Dandarhat. In the distance were the lights of Madras, and the ocean beyond them. Ariel felt Sharad shaking on his back.

"Are you going to fly?" Sharad whispered into his ear.

Ariel became anxious. Could he really rise into the air? It was easy to fly in a room, but now, in a storm, with Sharad on his back... What if he fell down in the middle of the courtyard?

The gong rang suddenly, not at all on schedule. An alarm! Ariel imagined Bharava's angry face, remembered his threats and rose above the roof.

He felt dizzy. His thoughts became confused.

Like an airplane making a circle over an airfield before taking its course, Ariel flew over the roof. There were shouts in the courtyard, followed by a gunshot. Lanterns flickered and a few windows lit up.

Through pouring rain, Ariel headed forward, flying with the wind blowing from south-east.

The courtyard flashed beneath him, the flat roofs, the park, the walls.

The wind carried Ariel toward the ocean. On the left, there was a mountain range, barely visible in the flashing lightning. Ahead was Madras. The fiery eye of the lighthouse burned in Fort St. George. Ariel was now flying over a sandy plain, so low that he could see the rice fields, and then more sand. The rain lashed at his body, the wind whistled in his ears and tugged at his hair.

A train crawled beneath them, its lights sparkling. There was a steamship out in the ocean. It was approaching the harbor and giving a warning signal.

They reached Madras. The small dirty river Cooum ran high with rain. Narrow crooked streets of the "Black city" were crowded with low brick houses mixed with bamboo cabins. The European portion of the city was well lit. Ariel and Sharad could hear the beeping of cars and tram bells. The dome of the observatory and nabob's palace rose above the city's roofs.

They flew over the botanical garden. In the light of streetlamps and lightning flashes they could see the coconut and date trees, Indian sycamores that could grow roots from their branches, bamboo groves, and coffee trees.

There were exclamations of surprise along the garden paths. Only then did Ariel realize how careless he was flying over the city. But he himself was so overwhelmed by the flight that he became confused. At times he thought it was a dream. Sharad was yelling something, but Ariel could not figure out what because of the noise of the rain and wind. Finally, Sharad shouted directly into his ear, "Those people have noticed us, dada!"

Instead of an answer, Ariel turned steeply west, to the mountains. He was getting tired. His entire body was covered in sweat and he was breathing heavily. But he had to get as far away as he could from Dandarhat and Madras.

The storm was almost over, the rain diminished, but the wind was still strong. Ariel summoned whatever energy he had. Sharad held on to him firmly, and Ariel could feel the warmth of his little friend on his back. He had to save him no matter what!

They flew through darkness and storm to meet their unknown destiny.

CHAPTER SEVEN. BODEN AND HESLON

The law office of Boden and Heslon – London, Citi, King William Street – was located next to the St. Mary Woolnoth Church.

From the office window one could see the statue of Holy Virgin in a niche, darkened by London fog and soot. The tolling of the church clock was louder than even the hissing and coughing of the antique office clock in a black worm-eaten wooden case of such enormous size that Boden and Heslon could have both fit into it. They were two dry, clean-shaven little old men in old-fashioned jackets who looked like twin brothers.

For thirty years they sat across from each other behind the writing desks that were old enough to belong in a museum, separated from the clerks by a glass partition. They could observe their employees through the glass and still discuss the firm's secret cases without worrying about eavesdropping. Although, they spoke very little, understanding each other almost without words.

Having read a letter, Boden inscribed a mysterious symbol in the corner and handed it to Heslon. The latter took his turn to read it, examined Boden's hieroglyph and wrote down a resolution for the clerk. Only in rare cases their opinions differed, but even then they only needed a few brief words or short phrases to reach an agreement.

Theirs was an old, well-known firm specializing in matters of inheritance, wills and guardianship. The firm serviced only wealthy clients. It was no wonder that Boden and Heslon managed to put away a fortune, whose size significantly exceeded the size of a usual retainer. But that side of business remained the firm's secret, kept in accounting books behind thick walls of fireproof safes.

That sunny morning, which was rare for London, Mister Boden sorted through the correspondence as usual and tossed the papers he finished reading onto the desk of his partner.

A heavy blue envelope was postmarked in Madras. Boden quickly tore it open and became absorbed in the letter, pursing his thin dry lips harder and harder as he read.

Having finished reading the letter, he turned on the radio. The announcer's voice was reading out stock prices, but Boden was not listening to him. The radio was turned on only to make certain that the clerks could not hear a single word from Boden's and Heslon's conversation. Apparently, a very important conference was about to take place between them, and Heslon leveled his owl-like, pale, round eyes at Boden.

But the announcer was wasting his time: Boden had yet to say anything. He silently threw the letter over to Heslon, who read it very carefully and once again leveled his whitish eyes at his partner. They sat that way for some time, as if conducting a silent conversation.

Indeed, much was exchanged between them during these few minutes. Or rather, each of them thought about the same thing, refreshing in his memory all the circumstances of one of their most profitable but also most complex cases – the Galton case.

Several years prior, an old client of Boden and Heslon died – a wealthy landlord and industrialist, baronet Sir Thomas Galton. He left two underage children – Aurelius and his sister Jane. According to the will, all of Thomas Galton's substantial real estate and a lion share of his liquid assets was left to his son Aurelius, with Boden and Heslon appointed as his guardians until his coming of age. The guardianship turned out to be a goldmine for them. Along with other members of the guardianship council, they managed the estate so deftly that their own fortunes grew swiftly year after year. But they could not abide by the fact that the moment the heirs came of age, this source of income would run out, and Aurelius would assume management of his somewhat diminished but still significant fortune. In case of Aurelius' death prior to coming of age, his property would go to his sister Jane, who was older than her brother and, thus, even closer to the end of the guardianship.

The most beneficial outcome for the clever guardians was a situation in which Aurelius remained alive, but became disabled by the time he came of age. Legally, it was possible if Aurelius became mentally incompetent and was officially certified as such. Boden and Heslon applied their efforts in that direction. They had placed their charges in mental institutions many times, where the bribed doctors skillfully turned normal children into mentally ill adults. However, it was not cheap. The Madras school of Dandarhat had more understanding people who could bring about the same results, as Boden and Heslon knew very well. Madras school had an additional advantage of being in distant India, where the guardianship council, with whom Boden and Heslon had a good working relationship, and, more importantly, a growing Jane could not follow Aurelius' life. When Aurelius was a small child, Boden himself took him to Dandarhat. As the school did not officially exist, the institution figuring prominently in the guardians' reports was a mythical sanatorium for emotionally unstable children. The forms, signatures and reports of that sanatorium were fabricated at Dandarhat.

Having taken the little Aurelius to Dandarhat, Mister Boden had a long conversation with the school's headmaster Piers-Bharava, giving him the following instructions: the life and physical health of Aurelius Galton must be preserved no matter what. As for his nervous system and his psyche, they had to be compromised to the limit. Aurelius was not to receive anything resembling a normal education. He was not to be developed mentally. He was not to be provided any practical knowledge, any notion of real life. Even if they failed to drive him mad, he was to be kept in the state of infantilism – a stage of development no more advanced than that of a small child.

Piers quickly understood what was being asked of him and promised to make Aurelius into a classical idiot. It took some time, but they also agreed on the price.

Completely satisfied, Boden returned to London. His entire report to his partner regarding his trip consisted of two words, "All right!" and Heslon did not ask about anything else.

Piers sent Boden and Heslon two official reports per year for the benefit of the guardianship council, as well as unofficial communications. At first, they were very comforting. But later, the following phrases became more and more prominent, "Unfortunately, Ariel-Aurelius is turning out to be a difficult student," and the partners knew very well what it meant.

They did not lose hope. At worst, if Aurelius did not become mad, they could still get him certified as incompetent. In each and every report to the council Boden and Heslon managed the mental retardation of their charge. When the time came to present a fully grown man to the medical experts, the council and the court, he wouldn't be able to answer the usual questions, "What day it is? What month? How old are you? What is your nationality and faith?" and so on. To each and every question he would invariably reply, "I don't know," and his deficiency would be obvious to all. The rest would be accomplished through the friendly relations with the medical experts and the guardianship council.

Years passed. There were only a few months left until Aurelius' birthday, when the ill-fated letter arrived and forced Boden to turn on the radio.

Piers informed them that Aurelius' studies at the Dandarhat school were complete, but, of course, he could remain there until his coming of age.

As "the mental state of Ariel-Aurelius Galton still, sadly, left much to be desired", he, Piers, was forced to subject him to a course of treatments by Professor Hyde. "Misters Boden and Heslon know what an experienced doctor and talented scientist he is. To my greatest dismay, even the interference by Professor Hyde did not have the desired effect upon Ariel's mental capacity, although the experiment was not entirely fruitless. Quite unexpectedly for all, including Professor Hyde, Ariel acquired an unusual and truly miraculous ability, which is hard to believe without witnessing – the ability to rise into the air without any mechanism. This divine gift makes Ariel very useful for the great purposes our organization pursues."

In the first draft of the letter Piers initially wrote "priceless", but then corrected it to the more cautious "very useful".

"If the respected Misters Boden and Heslon do not object, the TS and the SOK (which stood for Theosophical Society and the Society of Occult Knowledge) are prepared to immediately use Ariel for their purposes, naturally, after he is certified as a mentally incompetent person."

Finally, the radio announcer came in useful: moving closer to Heslon, Boden said, "Did Piers go mad?"

"It happens to those who constantly have to deal with crazy people," Heslon replied with a nod.

"In any case…" and without finishing the sentence, Boden started writing something on a telegraph slip. Having jotted down a few lines, he handed the slip to Heslon. It said, "Take no action until our instructions. Take all measures to guard him. Boden, Heslon."

Heslon nodded and handed the slip to the clerks through an opening in the partition, along with the address.

"One of us will have to go," Heslon said.

"Yes," Boden replied.

And the partners stared at each other, considering this new situation.

"Jane..." Boden said after a pause, redirecting his partner's thoughts.

"Yes," he replied.

And they became so ponderous, that even a yogi would have envied their concentration.

CHAPTER EIGHT. THE STUMBLING BLOCK

No question pertaining to Aurelius' fate could be discussed without considering his sister Jane. She was his sister and possible heiress. But most importantly – she was Jane. Her temper had caused the guardians many troubles and disappointments. She was their stumbling block, their constant obstacle. Boden and Heslon hated her.

Even as a child, Jane was particularly stubborn and disobedient. As she got older, she started demonstrating clear dislike and mistrust toward the guardians. Ever since Aurelius' departure to India, Boden and Heslon attempted to convince her that her brother was mentally ill, that he was being treated and that a meeting with him was impossible, for it could hurt him. But she remained unconvinced and repeated stubbornly, "I do not believe you. Where are you hiding him? I want to see him."

While Jane was under their guardianship, Boden and Heslon managed to control her more or less. But she was older than Aurelius and came of age a few months prior – the event she marked by the act of black ingratitude toward her guardians: Jane invited Boden's and Heslon's worst enemy, attorney George Dotaller, to manage her estate, giving him the power of attorney in all matters of her inheritance. The day before the arrival of Piers' letter, she did something so ill-mannered, that the honorable partners were struck to the very depth of their souls. She showed up at the office with her new advisor and caused a real scandal, demanding loudly enough for the clerks to hear to disclose the location of her brother and threatening to sue.

Boden was outraged and protested "against this rude interference in their guardianship rights."

"We are obligated to report our actions solely to the guardianship council," he said.

"In that case, I shall appeal to the council myself and make them tell me where my brother is!" the girl exclaimed and left with her attorney without even offering to shake hands.

Jane could get her way. Having to go to India and find her brother would not stop her. What if she found him playing the role of a flying miracle under the guidance of theosophists and occultists! It was beginning to smell like a scandal. Her departure had to be delayed no matter what, and in the meantime…

Boden pulled his eyes away from the gaze of his companion and quickly jotted down the text of a new secret telegram to Piers, "Hide Aurelius in a secure location. Be ready to receive his sister. Boden, Heslon."

Piers knew all the circumstances. Boden made it all clear to Piers when he delivered Aurelius to him.

At the guardianship council, Jane can only receive the address of the fictional "sanatorium school for mentally ill children". Of course, she will not find the school. But if the Dandarhat people were so stupid as to start demonstrating the flying man, the news of this miracle would spread not only through all of India, but also all over the world. Once in India, Jane would want to see this wonder. Suppose she would not recognize Aurelius, for he was now a grown young man, and the last time she saw him he was a child. But still, every possibility of their meeting must be eliminated.

Before Boden tossed the telegram form to Heslon, a clerk handed him a telegram that was only just received, "Aurelius vanished. Organizing search. Piers."

At first Boden did not understand what he was reading. The telegram that Aurelius "vanished" was received before he even had a chance to send one about hiding him. Was there a mistake at the telegraph office? But no, the phrase "organizing search" spoke differently.

"He flew away after all! Idiots!" Boden hissed and threw the telegram across with such a desperate gesture, that it nearly hit Heslon in the face.

Heslon read it and they once again stared at each other like two owls.

The trip to India was unavoidable. It was not going to be cheap. They would also have to spend a substantial sum to locate Aurelius.

Neither Boden nor Heslon liked spending money, even if it was from Aurelius' account. After all, his account was their account. Could they transfer the expense to others?

CHAPTER NINE. THE HUMAN ANT HILL

Jane was very surprised when Boden showed up to see her on the evening of the same day.

"My threats must have worked," she thought, inviting the visitor to sit.

"We had a disagreement yesterday, Jane," Boden said, taking a seat. "But you must understand me. I am not working alone. If I satisfied your demands and gave you Aurelius' address, my partner would have been offended, thinking that you did not trust him in the choice of conditions in which your brother is kept."

"I care not at all whether your partner might or might not be offended. I am Aurelius' sister and have the right to know everything about my brother and to see him," Jane objected.

"I completely agree," Boden said peaceably. After a pause, he exclaimed, "Listen, Jane! It grieves me greatly that we have disagreements."

"Whose fault is it, Mister Boden?"

"If we concealed the location of your brother from you until now, it was only following the recommendations of the doctors who believe that your meeting could be harmful to his health. Any sort of surprise could be dangerous to him, even if it is a pleasant one."

"I don't believe you."

Boden sighed with the air of a man being undeservedly insulted.

"Please understand, to fulfill your whim…"

"My whim? You call a sister's desire to find out about the fate of her brother a whim?"

"But in fulfilling your wish, I could cause harm to Aurelius, for whom I am responsible as a guardian. And if I refuse you, I only cause your anger and suspicion. This damages the good name, honor and pride of our company. So, you can have your way. You are of age and you are Aurelius' sister. You are capable of being responsible for your actions. I shall tell you where Aurelius is, but on one condition. If you go to see him, I must be present during your meeting. My duties as a guardian bind me to it."

Jane did not want to travel with Boden, but his suggestion simplified matters: he would make it easier to find her brother, and she did not object.

"This trip," Boden continued, "is associated with the loss of time and money, and its purpose is solely to satisfy your whim... your wish..."

"I shall cover all expenses," Jane replied quickly. "Not only yours, but also those of Mister Dotaller, who is coming with me."

Boden winced. This Dotaller again! But the guardian knew Jane well enough – there was no arguing with her.

He had to agree.

"Shall I order tickets on an ocean liner for you?" he asked.

"I shall order them myself, but not on a ship. We are taking an airplane."

"Are you that impatient? It will cost a lot."

"It will cost *me* a lot, not you."

Boden pondered. He was a bit scared to fly on an airplane. But the sooner they arrived at Madras, the better. He said nothing about Aurelius' escape or "flight". It was too unusual, too impossible. Perhaps Piers did go mad. This made it especially important to investigate everything on the spot.

"It will cost a lot," Boden repeated. "It's nowhere nearby."

"France? Switzerland? Italy?" Jane asked.

"India," Boden replied.

"India!" Jane exclaimed in surprise. "Yes, it's a long way." She thought about it. "It doesn't matter. I shall lease a passenger airplane."

After Boden's departure Jane thought long and hard. So that was where Boden and Heslon sent her brother! There had to be a reason. India! With its climate that was dreadful for Europeans, malaria, plague, cholera, snakes, tigers... That was almost everything Jane knew about India.

She went into her library and started setting aside books. The girl's impatience to get to know this country was so great, that she opened them at random and read. Her head became filled with chaos. It was all so complex, unusual, confusing... A mix of races, tribes, languages, dialects, castes, religions... Swarthy Aryans, Indians, coffee-colored Dravidians, ebony natives. Aryan languages included Hindustani, Bengali, Marathi; Dravidian languages – Telugu, Tamil, Tibet-Burman. There were more than two hundred dialects. The castes included Brahmins – the priests, Kshatriya – warriors, Vaishya – traders and manufacturers, Shudra – farmers, with internal caste divisions, their total number reaching 2,578. There were hereditary castes of physicians, confectioners, gardeners, potters, astrologers, clowns, acrobats, poets, vagrants, mourners, beggars, gravediggers, executioners, collectors of cow manure, drummers. They probably all had their own unique costumes. What a colorful mix! "Pure castes" were those of confectioners, sellers of perfume and betel. What was betel? Barbers and potters... They were all at odds with each other and afraid to touch each other. The masons despised the chimney sweeps, the chimney sweeps despised the curriers, the curriers despised the collectors of carrion. Brahmins, Buddhists, Christians, Muslims were grouped into endless sects and religious societies. "Thirty-three million gods," the book said. "Six million widows." Why so many? Ah, there it was, "Widows in India are not allowed to marry for the second time. There are a hundred thousand widows under the age of ten, and three hundred thousand – under the age of fifteen. A widow gets her head shaved, her glass hand and ankle bracelets are broken, and the late husband's relatives take away her jewelry."

It was a terrifying life of half-imprisonment and half-mourning. Many widows could not stand it and committed suicide.

None of Jane's books said anything about new developments in India, new people, and newly empowered women. The impression she received about the country was that of an enormous, chaotic, swarming human ant hill. And somewhere in the midst of three hundred million of black, saffron and coffee-colored ants her brother was lost. Jane shuddered, pushed aside the books and called Dotaller.

CHAPTER TEN. HOMELESS BEGGARS

Ariel was gasping for breath. Drops of rain on his face mixed with drops of sweat. He felt he could no longer fly with a burden on his back. He had to rest.

A forest loomed in the darkness beneath, with a paler-colored area next to it, probably sand.

They landed by a banyan tree, whose roots crawled down its trunk and formed a dark network of tangled coils at the bottom. A copse of young bamboo surrounded the tree. It was a secluded corner where they could rest, without worrying about being seen.

Breathing heavily, Ariel untied the towel. Sharad hopped down off his back and immediately fell to the ground before Ariel, trying to hug his legs and worship his rescuer like a god.

Ariel smiled sadly and said, pulling the boy to his feet, "I am not a god, Sharad. You and I are poor, homeless escapees. Let's settle down here and rest. We were able to get some ways away."

Sharad was somewhat disappointed by Ariel's explanation. It would have been nice to have a god for a friend. But he was too tired to think about all that.

They crawled deep into the tangle of roots, not even worrying about snakes and insects.

Ariel carefully tucked the rolled-up towel under Sharad's head and the boy fell asleep instantly.

Despite his fatigue, Ariel could not fall asleep. He was too agitated.

The wind scattered the clouds. Large stars sparkled in the sky. The moon was setting behind the dark forest. The last few light white clouds passed across its disk, like dreams. A sweetly spicy fragrance of flowers floated in from somewhere, perhaps from a nearby garden. It reached deep into his troubled heart, making him alarmed at the thought of possible human habitation nearby.

A gust of wind pulled the strip of white fog from the surface of the earth.

And Ariel, much to his displeasure, saw that they landed in a not at all deserted area. Beyond the band of sand, a river glittered like black steel. The flickering light of lanterns on boats tied at the dock were reflected in the water, and all of the darkness now seemed to be concentrated in the thick foliage of trees on the opposite bank. The moon became hidden behind the trees. And only some large star, perhaps the planet Jupiter, watched the sleeping land like a night sentinel, surrounded by a multitude of smaller stars scattered all over the sky.

This quiet landscape had a soothing effect. Ariel's eyelids drooped. Not letting go of Sharad's warm hand, Ariel dozed off, leaning against the snake-like roots.

In his half-sleep he imagined new countries, some strange unknown lands, where the days under clear skies were akin the gazes of wide open eyes, and the nights were like timid shadows trembling under lowered eyelashes, where snakes did not sting and people did not torture and kill each other.

Did he read that somewhere? In the book of life, or in a collection of a Bengali poet perhaps. The dream of a dream...

Something prickled his eyes. Ariel opened them and saw the old banyan tree, whose leaves were dressed in a thin veil of morning fog, the red beams of the rising sun shining through it. The dew sparkled like gold on bamboo leaves.

A song sounded from the left. Ariel turned his head. Through the tree trunks he saw a pond with a stone staircase descending to the water, surrounded by coconut trees.

In the pond, a stocky man was engaged in his morning bath. He covered his ears and performed the required number of dips. Next to him, another man, probably a Brahmin, who was afraid of desecration even in the purifying water, pushed aside the leaves and twigs on the surface and dove in at once. The third man did not dare to enter the pond, he settled for wetting a towel and squeezing the water onto his head.

Some descended the steps slowly, others, mumbling the morning prayer, dove into the pond from the top steps. Yet others enjoyed a sponge bath on the bank, some changed their bathing clothes for fresh daily garments, some picked flowers in a nearby meadow.

At the far end of the pond ducks fed on water snails and cleaned their feathers.

Ariel thought he landed in the jungle, but it turned out that he was surrounded by people.

An occasional bee flew by, birdsong could be heard, and someone was singing by the river. Sharad was still asleep.

Ariel picked a clump of clay from a puddle and started rubbing it over his face, neck, arms and legs.

A gong rang somewhere, possibly in a temple. The familiar sound woke Sharad instantly. He sat up quickly, looked around in confusion, and saw unfamiliar surroundings and a smiling young man with chocolate-colored skin.

Sharad became frightened and was about to cry.

"Don't be afraid, Sharad, it's me," Ariel said gently.

Sharad fell to the ground before him.

The day before Ariel could fly, and now he turned from a white man into a dark-skin Dravidian. Only a god could do that.

"Get up, Sharad. Look, I just smeared some clay on my skin to keep from attracting attention with my pale skin color. Remember: we are beggars, walking along roads and asking for alms."

"Walking? Why not flying? Flying is much more interesting."

"Because if I fly, they will catch me like a bird and put me in a cage."

"Then turn them into birds or dogs, *dada!*" Sharad exclaimed.

Ariel laughed and gave up.

"Come on, Sharad."

They climbed out of their hiding place and stumbled along the road, pitted by the prior night's downpour. In the morning sun, the puddles shone like red gold.

There was a live fence of prickly plants along the road and a small pond beyond, covered with green water plants. A black-skinned bearded man stood in the water up do his waist brushing his teeth with the chewed-up end of a branch. He glanced at Ariel and Sharad indifferently and continued his ablutions.

A tall Kabulivala – the dweller of distant mountains in his wide robe – passed them on the road. A canvas sack hung behind his back and he was carrying baskets with grapes, raisins and nuts. He was hurrying to reach a village market.

Ariel and Sharad stepped off the roads, as pariahs would, knelt and started singing.

The Kabulivala set one of his baskets on the ground and threw them a bunch of grapes. Ariel and Sharad bowed to him. When he passed, Sharad ran to get the grapes, grabbed them hungrily and brought them to Ariel.

A buffalo passed, drawing a creaky cart. A naked boy with a shaved head, save for a clump of hair at the top, rode on its back. The old man in the cart saw the beggars and threw a rice cake to Sharad.

"We have food now," Ariel said.

After breakfast they continued along the road. A few sod-covered cabins were scattered through a guava grove ahead. Their walls were sealed with clay. The market was already bustling in a clearing in front of the village. Sellers of fruit, cheese, chilled water, flower garlands, fish, and dried flowers loudly invited passersby to sample their wares, half-naked children crowded around the sellers of toy whistles made of palm leaves, painted sticks, wooden clappers, and little glass dolls.

An Indian in an enormous turban, as thin and dry as a skeleton, sat under a bael tree playing a flute, his cheeks bulging. Snakes rose from his flat basket, rocking back and forth.

The crowd surrounded the snake charmer, albeit keeping some distance. A thin boy walked around the circle of spectators with a wooden cup, and peasants dropped small change into it – no more than a few anna[v]. Rupees could be found only in the pockets of the wealthiest peasants.

Another snake charmer settled nearby – a fat man with a black beard. As he played a long bassoon with a wide opening, he puffed his cheeks so much that they looked as if they would burst.

Women in colorful sari and yashmaks, with bracelets tinkling on their arms and legs, crowded near the sellers of scarves and colorful fabrics.

"Have mercy on me, good people! May God help you! Spare me a handful of your plenty," repeated a blind beggar with a wooden cup in his hand.

Acrobats writhed, vagrants sang, flutes played, drums thundered, goats bleated, donkeys roared, children screamed...

"Bracelets, who wants bracelets?" the seller of glass and copper bracelets shouted, inviting the women.

Sharad's eyes went wide. He pulled Ariel toward a group of children surrounding a simple toy display. Sharad enviously watched a little girl blowing a brand new red whistle and clearly forgetting everything else in the world.

Ariel too was captivated by the sight. After the mind-numbing silence and monotony of Dandarhat, this blinding light, multi-voice noise, bold, bright colors, people's movements, hot wind fluttering the scarves, sari and yashmaks, the flags, and the tree leaves filled him with unfamiliar excitement and intoxicated him. Like Sharad, he was drunk with the sight of life.

A car horn sounded abruptly from the road, obscuring other sounds. A mud-splattered car slowly made its way through the crowds toward the market. There were several Englishmen in white European suits riding in the car.

Ariel regained all of his caution. He firmly clasped Sharad's hand.

The car stopped. Two sahibs with photo cameras sliced into the crowd that parted respectfully before them, leaving a wide empty space. They were headed straight toward Ariel.

"A chase!" Ariel thought in terror and pulled Sharad toward the grove. But it wasn't easy to push through the heavy crowd, while the sahibs were practically on their heels. They were looking around as if searching for someone.

Ariel grabbed Sharad and flew up into the air.

An explosion of a bomb from hell could not have caused a greater commotion in the crowd. The entire market seemed to merge into one creature, screaming with shock and terror. Many fell to the ground, covering their heads with their capes and hands.

The thin snake charmer dropped his long flute, and it fell into the basket with the snakes. The snakes hissed and started crawling out and away. The towers of acrobats crumbled like houses of cards. A barber abandoned his client and dove into the pond, still holding his scissors and comb. People pushed and shoved each other, overturning baskets and tents, as they crawled under the carts to hide. Boys clapped their hands and screamed in delight.

The sahibs stood there with their mouths hanging open and their faces looking dumbstruck.

When the commotion settled down some, one of the sahibs, Mister Lynton, said to his companion, "Are you still going to deny that levitation exists?"

"India is indeed a land of wonders," the other answered, "unless… unless we fell victim to mass hypnosis. It is a pity that I did not photograph the flight. But I was so overwhelmed…"

CHAPTER ELEVEN. "LET'S BE HONEST – WE WERE BOTH WRONG."

Mister Lynton sent a column about the unusual incident witnessed by a number of people to a Madras newspaper. The article was published with a note from the editor, "Our special correspondent visited the location of the incident and questioned other witnesses, who confirmed the facts outlined by Mister Lynton in his article. Apparently, we are dealing either with a clever trick or with a new wingless flying device. This mysterious case continues to be investigated. The identity of the flying man and the boy who accompanied him has yet to be established."

This news was published by other newspapers and inspired much agitation and debate.

Indian newspapers siding with the progressive religious society *Brahmo-Samadge* laughed at the easily-fooled public, "Can a sensible twentieth century man truly believe that some youth kidnapped a boy in broad daylight, in the middle of a crowd, like a hawk snatching a chicken, and flew away with him?"

It must be mentioned that most witnesses were convinced that the young man indeed kidnapped the child.

The newspapers and magazines of the conservative "faithful" Brahmin sects used this unusual story to whip up religious fanaticism. They wrote about the great mysteries of the yogi, of levitation, and of miracles, portraying the unknown young man as nearly the new incarnation of a deity that came to earth to strengthen the impaired religion and shame the infidels.

The English theosophical newspapers were reluctant to express their thoughts on the subject, waiting for a directive from the London center. But the editors were inclined to think that it would be in the best interest of the English colonial rule in India to support the miracle version of the event. At the very least, the disputes and arguments within the Indian population were considered a "positive" trend: the more people argued, the easier it was to rule them.

A prominent Bengali scientist Ragupati declined to give a direct answer to the inquiries of *Brahmo-Samadge*, "A scientist can only express his opinion only about the facts he himself can verify in appropriate conditions. I can only say that I have never witnessed levitation, and that the modern scientist does not have even a hypothetical explanation for the possibility of such phenomena."

When Bharava-Piers read the column about the incident at the fair, he squeezed his head between his hands.

"It's Ariel and Sharad. So that's where they went!" And Piers thought in terror about the fit Brownlow would have at the news.

The storm followed without delay.

Mister Brownlow came to see Piers the same day. Piers has never seen the leader of the Indian theosophists so enraged.

Brownlow nearly beat Piers, threatened to kick him out of Dandarhat, called him a simpleton and a bungler.

"You took the responsibility upon yourself. The fault is entirely yours. Where is your vaunted chain of hypnosis that was supposed to keep Ariel in place better than a steel chain? What are we to tell Boden and Heslon? Or the London center? How are we to handle the newspaper fuss? To let such a trump card out of your hands!"

When Brownlow got tired of yelling and calmed down a little, Piers said, "At least now we know, if not the exact location, the area where Ariel is at. He did not fly away as far as I expected. Apparently, with Sharad, Ariel cannot fly as quickly, and he won't leave Sharad behind. We shall catch them."

"Catch them!" Brownlow interrupted him. "Catch the birds that broke out of their cage. We would have to make an army of flying captors, and that is not possible."

"But people catch birds with food traps," Piers objected. "Ariel and Sharad need food and water. We shall send out hundreds of people, if necessary, promise rewards to peasants, inform the population. I admit, Ariel managed to deceive and trick me. It is my fault. But who could have thought that he could pretend so well? It is my fault and I will not spare my own money to correct this error. Boden and Heslon will help. I have already informed them and received a telegram that Boden is traveling here by airplane. When Ariel and Sharad are back here, it will be easy to bribe the newspapers and the witnesses, and the entire thing will be made to look like a prank, a mystification, a newspaper publicity stunt. When they forget it all…"

"We will start demonstrating Ariel, and the entire story will be remembered again. No, the flying man is lost for Dandarhat. Ariel and Sharad must be captured but only to make certain that no one finds out about Dandarhat and what exactly it does. The school could be shut down and we…"

"We could end up in court? I hope things won't come to this. London won't allow it. A trial would compromise not only the Indian viceroy, but also the English government. What are Dandarhat's purposes? Whose instructions do we follow? Do you honestly think I will remain silent about all this if I have to stand before a judge?"

"You will."

"I shall tell everything as it is."

"You won't do it, Piers."

"I will. I would have nothing to lose. They know as much in London. I shall disclose enough to make the entire world gasp."

"Don't forget, Piers, that you too had a bit of history before finding safe haven at Dandarhat. You were spared prison and servitude in hopes that you would be an obedient and silent caretaker."

"Spared prison for my own crimes, only to send me there for someone else's? And what about you, prophet of all-encompassing love, tenderness and mercy? Don't you think I know about your career? Rest assured, I have made some inquiries about you. Not to mention your beneficial activities at Dandarhat. How many children were kidnapped from their parents on your orders? How many were killed and disfigured, how many committed suicide? I have it all written down. Am I to be the one to pay for it all? Am I to be the *only* one?"

For some time they stared at each other silently, like two roosters before another fight.

But sensibility triumphed. Brownlow clapped Piers on the shoulder and said with a mocking smile, "We were both wrong! Let's not argue. We need to find a way out of this situation, Bharava-*babu*."

"About time!" Piers exclaimed.

"As for Ariel, we will most likely have to get rid of him."

"Finish him off, you mean," Piers said.

"Once we lay our hands on him."

They started discussing the plan of action.

CHAPTER TWELVE. AIRBORNE STOWAWAYS

Having risen above the market, Ariel flew toward the grove. Blood thudded in his temples. Sharad's weight was tugging on his arms and making the flight difficult. To better slice through the air, Ariel flew almost horizontally, clutching Sharad to his chest.

Ariel did his best to fly over the woods, avoiding open spaces. But the woods soon ended. There were fields almost to the horizon. Factory smokestacks towered here and there.

Ariel and Sharad watched as the peasants working in the fields raised their heads and stood there with their mouths hanging open. Some fell to the ground or ran away. Sharad was very amused by all that. He stuck his tongue out at them and dangled his feet, but all Ariel could think about was whether he had enough energy to make it to the grove he could see in the distance.

Suddenly, Ariel heard what sounded like buzzing of a giant bee. Glancing back, he saw an approaching airplane flying rather low and not very fast. Was it after him? Ariel was just about to drop to the ground like a rock, but quickly realized that Piers would not chase after him on an airplane. After all, how would he catch him in the air? But the airplane could contain Piers' spies. What if people started shooting at him from the airplane?

While Ariel pondered all this, the airplane came very close. The pilot couldn't help but notice Ariel and Sharad. Ariel decided to go up and let the airplane go beneath him.

As it was passing by under their feet, Sharad shouted, "*Dada*, land on the wing!"

Ariel did not hear Sharad's voice over the noise of the engine, but he came to the same decision on his own. The wing was the best place to hide, if someone decided to shoot at them. Speeding up, Ariel lowered them toward the surface of the wing, holding Sharad tightly.

Only when Sharad grabbed a protruding ledge on the side Ariel relaxed his arms and "mentally sat down" on the wing, causing the airplane to dip a little. He could finally rest. Out of caution, he "suspended" his body and tied Sharad to himself with the towel. They could now travel as airborne stowaways.

Sharad was delighted. They finally had a firm support under them. Although, the metal surface did become so heated from the sun that it was nearly scorching to the skin, but it was a small inconvenience to bear. The most important thing was that they were flying to the north toward Bengal, along the shore of the Bengal Bay. This was excellent. They could travel far without wasting energy. This must have been a postal-passenger airplane following the Madras-Calcutta route.

Ariel was worried about one thing: what would the passengers do if they notice him and Sharad? He remained alert.

No more than half an hour passed when a head in a pilot's helmet and goggles appeared out of the cockpit, near the edge of the right wing. Would it be followed by a hand with a revolver? But the head soon disappeared and did not return. Perhaps the people inside were discussing what to do. The pilot must have noticed the nudge and the increase in the airplane's weight.

A lighthouse appeared in the distance, followed by the round dome of the observatory. There was something very familiar about it... Suddenly, Ariel gasped – he recognized Madras.

Ariel had no life experience and no practical knowledge of any kind. He made a fateful error! The airplane was not traveling to the north – it was going south, to Madras. Of course! The ocean was to the left of them. He blamed himself for not noticing that.

Ariel grabbed the puzzled Sharad and rushed downward. Fortunately, there were thick copses of bamboo and reeds beneath them.

Deafened by the roaring of the engines, they could not hear each other for some time. Only when their ears stopped ringing did Ariel explain to Sharad why they abandoned the airplane so suddenly.

"We'll do better next time. We'll wait for fog or twilight and land onto the plane flying north. I won't make the same mistake twice."

They were hungry but they were used to that at Dandarhat. Sharad chewed on the reed shoots. Afraid to end up in the hands of their enemies, they remained in their hiding place.

By evening the sky became covered with clouds. It rained at night and heavy fog rolled in by morning. Suddenly, they heard the humming of engines in the fog. Ariel and Sharad, connected by the towel, rose into the air. Landing on the wing in the fog was not easy and far from safe. The airplane nearly ran into them and passed them, when Ariel dashed off to the side. He had to strain to catch up with it.

He finally managed. Ariel carefully lowered them onto the wing causing the slightest list.

They flew almost all day, suffering from the heat, thirst and hunger, but every hour, every minute took them further away from the hateful Dandarhat and the fearsome Piers.

In the evening they got caught in a thunderstorm. The airplane was pulled this way and that. It dropped and rose, seemingly on waves made out of air.

During one particularly strong gust of wind Ariel and Sharad were knocked off the wing. Ariel had no energy to chase after the airplane and they headed down.

"I think we made it far enough away this time, Sharad," Ariel said.

CHAPTER THIRTEEN. VISHNU AND PARIAHS

While still in the air, they saw the ruins of a long building without a roof. Ariel and Sharad landed on a pile of gravel in one of the rooms of the building, spooking an entire cloud of bats hiding in the corners. The bats fluttered about for some time until they finally settled down. The escapees found a spot protected from rain and wind, huddled together and fell asleep.

Ariel was the first one to wake up at dawn. He rose, trying not to wake up Sharad. He climbed out through a break in the wall and looked around.

The sun was not up yet. Wisps of light fog stretched above the earth like nighttime ghosts, startled by the first morning breeze. All the plants were covered with large dewdrops. The ruins of the awkward angular building made the landscape gloomy. The ugly ashat tree reached through gaping cracks in the wall with its thick grasping roots. More wall segments rose between flowering shrubs here and there. Two crumbling pillars indicated where the gates used to be. An alley of shishu trees went from the pillars toward the river bank. There were small hillocks in the shadow of centuries' old deodars that looked like graves. A pond with muddy banks glittered through the fog. Water poured out of it in small streams and its bottom housed the roots of a coriander. The scent of the coriander blossoms filled the entire garden. Beyond the garden was a small corn patch with a straw-roofed cabin on one side. The cabin's clay walls were darkened by the recent rains.

Dawn colored the fog in crimson. Birds twittered, crows woke up in their nests. The first ray of sun turned a dewdrop on a leaf into a diamond. Ariel became mesmerized by the sparkling dot. But suddenly, it vanished. The thirsty sun drank it all up. Ariel felt sad. Beauty and joy were so short-lived... He sat down on a rock and pondered.

Sounds and rustlings of the approaching day kept him from focusing.

An old man in a *dhoti* stepped out from the cabin near the corn field and began his daily morning chore – covering the walls of his home with fresh clay, while humming a tune.

Shortly, a teenage girl emerged from the cabin. She was dressed in a grayish sari that must have been blue at some point. The girl's black hair was braided into long plaits. She was carrying a copper basin and a small pot. The bracelets around the girl's wrists and ankles and the dishes in her hands rang with every step.

The girl glanced fearfully at the ruins. Ariel was becoming worried. Could these people have seen him, when he landed with Sharad?

The girl walked up to the creek and started scrubbing the dishes with sand.

"Come here, good boy," Ariel was startled by a gentle voice. He turned and saw through the lace of thinning fog a young man standing in the water up to his waist at the opposite side of the pond, and on the shore next to him – an enormous ox with gentle obedient eyes. As if responding to the man's invitation, the ox sighed noisily and slowly walked into the pond, its broad chest making a small wave in front of him. The young man started thoroughly washing the ox, the animal snorting with pleasure and slowly nodding its head.

Was it the young man who caused the old man and the girl to glance furtively at the ruins? The man and the girl did exchange a few glances but did not say a single word to each other.

Having finished bathing the ox, the man led it out of the pond, glanced at the girl one more time and, patting the ox's glistening hide, walked away down an overgrown path. The girl's eyes followed him until he vanished beyond the grove.

"*Dada*! Ariel, *dada*! Where are you?" Sharad's voice sounded. He woke up, did not find Ariel next to him, became worried, and ran out looking for him. "Ah, here you are, *dada*! I am hungry, *dada*! Very hungry!"

Ariel saw that the girl noticed Sharad, dropped the pot she was scrubbing and, abandoning her dishes, ran to the cabin. Her sari fluttered in the wind over her shoulders and back, the hem flew up baring her strong dark-skinned legs, and her bracelets jangled loudly. The old man looked at the girl, then shook the clay off his hands and also vanished inside the cabin.

"Look what you've done, Sharad," Ariel said, rising from behind a shrub. "They saw us."

"Forgive me, *dada*, but I became so scared when I didn't see you."

"What are we going to do now? Run away? Fly away?"

"As you wish," Sharad replied obediently. "But I am very, very hungry. I have never been this hungry, even my legs are shaking. We haven't eaten all day yesterday and all of last night. Maybe they'll find a handful of rice for us."

"Piers' spies are unlikely to live in this desolate place. And we can always fly away. Sharad is right. We should ask these peasants for some food," Ariel thought. He too felt hungry and weak. He couldn't fly far in this state.

While he thought about it, the door of the cabin opened and the old man appeared in the doorway. He had a wooden platter and two bowls in his hands and a woven straw mat under his arm. The girl, dressed in a new red sari, was peeking over his shoulder. She was carrying a wreath of flowers. They solemnly walked along the edge of the corn field toward the ruins, the old man leading the way and the girl following. Ariel and Sharad waited silently to see what would happen next. About seventy paces from them, the old man halted. The girl took the mat from under his arm and spread it on the ground, and the old man placed the platter onto the mat. Then they both bowed to Ariel.

"Greetings, oh messenger of heaven! Allow my granddaughter to touch her forehead to your feet. Bless us. He who is above all people will not be defiled by the closeness of the rejected ones. But if we are unworthy of your blessing, please, give us the joy of accepting this food from us, which we offer you with all of our hearts!"

Ariel did not understand why the old man was honoring him in this way. Sharad, his hungry eyes fixed on the platter, nudged Ariel and whispered, "Let's go, *dada*! I see fried rice and milk!"

Ariel walked toward the old man. The man and his granddaughter walked backwards to keep the distance.

"Thank you, kind people," Ariel said, having reached the mat with the platter. "Why do you walk away from us? We shall be happy to share breakfast with you. Sharad, take the platter and the mat. Carry it toward the house!" and he added quietly, "Don't eat until I tell you."

The old man and his granddaughter stopped, still bowing. When Ariel and Sharad approached, the girl blushed, held the wreath out to Ariel with shaking hands and mumbled something.

Ariel bowed, took the wreath from her and put it around his neck.

When they reached the cabin, the old man beamed and led them around his home, taking him to a small porch. The wall of the house, adjacent to the porch was covered with soot from lanterns.

The girl spread the mat once again. Sharad placed the dishes on the floor, and everyone settled around them.

"Bring some sugar molasses, *luchi* and more rice, Lolita," the old man said. But the girl kept gazing at Ariel as if entranced, as he looked back into her big brown eyes, lined with soot. "Lolita!" the old man repeated. She gave a start and ran to carry out his order. "Please accept this food from the hands of the unworthy slave!"

Sharad did not have to be asked twice. Ariel too attacked his share with gusto.

"It's a pity we cannot flavor the rice with the juice of green mango," the old man continued. "I have some mango trees on my plot," and he pointed, "but I am too old to get the fruit."

Ariel looked in the direction where the old man pointed.

"Tell me, *babu*, what is your name?" he asked.

"Nizmat," the old man said, moved by the fact that his guest addressed him as a father.

"Are there any people nearby?" Ariel asked.

"Just the young Ishvar who lives beyond the grove with his blind mother."

"He must be the young man I saw," Ariel thought. "There is no need to be afraid of him. He looked like a kind man. He was so gentle with his ox."

Ariel guessed the distance to the trees and said, "I'll bring you a few pieces of fruit."

Not bothering to get up, he rose into the air seated, went above the house and flew toward the trees.

He felt an unusual lightness.

For the first time, he was flying under the open sky without anyone to carry. He was suddenly overcome by such delight that he was ready to sing and tumble in the air. As he flew by an old sprawling tree, he dove in the air, pulled off several leaves and threw them around himself, enjoying the game. He then approached the mango tree, did a circle over its large heavy leaves, descended and, hanging vertically in the air, started gathering the orange-yellow fruit the size of a goose egg. Having picked a few he dove through the air toward the porch, frightening pigeons on the roof and a peacock by the steps.

Nizmat was sprawled face-down on the mat. Lolita sat on the floor surrounded by the scattered bowls, rice cakes and wooden platters she must have dropped. Only Sharad was laughing and slapping his knees, his face flushed and his eyes bright. What a commotion his friend had caused!

Ariel himself felt awkward, seeing the girl's dismay and the old man's astonishment.

"Forgive me, sir, I must have frightened you," he said.

"Oh the light, caressing my eyes! Light, bringing joy to my heart! I am filled with your joy! Oh, master of heaven! You made me a part of your glory! Oh, Vishnu, embodied in Rama and Krishna! Are my eyes, that haven't seen joy in so long, being honored by your tenth incarnation?" and Nizmat, still kneeling, held his hands out to Ariel.

"I am... No, no, Nizmat-*babu*, I am not Vishnu! I am an ordinary mortal man, just like you. I can only fly. I was made that way against my will. You know full well that people can fly in airplanes, and you don't consider them gods. Dragonflies can fly, and flies, and birds..."

But Ariel could see that the old man did not believe him, because he could not give up the joy of seeing a living deity. Perhaps, he shouldn't have tried to take this joy away from him.

"Very well! Consider me whoever you wish, but treat me like an ordinary man. I am ordering you! Sit next to me and eat. And Lolita should sit and eat too. And tell me about your life."

"As you wish!" the old man replied. "Sit, Lolita," he told his granddaughter. "Eat and may your heart rejoice!"

Nizmat started telling about himself.

He was the lowest of pariahs. Temple doors were closed to him. He could not take water from community wells. He had to step off the road, even if it was into mud or into a swamp, to put the required number of paces between himself and people of higher castes or people from the higher level of his own caste, to keep from defiling them with his breath or even with his gaze. He and his family had been hungry all their lives. His eldest son, the joy of his eyes and consolation of his old age, became sick when he turned twenty. His wife called a village healer, and the charlatan spent all night branding the patient with hot iron and shouting incantations. But the evil spirit possessing his son was stronger, and he died by morning. Such was the will of the gods. Nizmat's wife, second son and his family – wife and children – all died from cholera, malaria, and hunger. Only his granddaughter Lolita was left. Her husband died too.

"Lolita is a widow?" Ariel asked in surprise. "How old is she?"

"She will be fifteen soon. She has been a widow for three years."

"But why is Lolita not dressed in the widow's white? Why is her hair not shaved? Why does she still wear her bracelets? Weren't the relatives of her husband supposed to take them away or break them?" Sharad asked, who knew the local traditions better than Ariel.

"We are too poor to observe all the rituals and traditions, and Lolita's late husband had no family," Nizmat replied. "Our neighbor Ishvar loves Lolita," the girl lowered her gaze and blushed when he said that, "and wants to marry her. But his mother does not want her son to marry a widow as some people do when they scorn the old ways. The blind woman still remembers the time when widows were burned alive along with the bodies of their dead husbands. She was nearly burned herself, but the sahibs interfered. But the woman firmly obeys the old law: no widow must marry again. That is why there are so many widows in our country," Nizmat sighed. "And my bloodline shall fade."

Ariel thought about it. This was not something he was taught at Dandarhat. Ariel wanted to ask whether Lolita loved Ishvar back, but didn't. He wasn't sure whether he was afraid to embarrass Lolita any further or to hear the affirmative answer from her lips.

To change the subject, he asked, "What are these ruins?"

"There used to be an indigo factory here," Nizmat replied. "The owner was a sahib, a cruel man who knew how to turn the blood of his workers into the bright blue indigo paint. He bargained with the local raja Rajkumar, and the raja took the land away from us, peasants, and gave it to the sahib. To keep from starving, the peasants deprived of their land were forced to work at the factory, setting aside their caste differences. I used to work there too. Several Muslim peasants from another village demanded their fields back, for their land was taken away too to grow indigo. The factory owner employed not only men, but also women, the elderly and children seven years of age and older. Workers kept dying. The sahib died too. Some said he died of fever, some – that it was a snake bite. There were also rumors that he was strangled by one of the Muslim workers. Of the three villages the only ones left alive are my granddaughter and I, and the blind Tara with her son. The migrant workers left. The factory fell apart. The brush and flowers cover more and more of the ruins. Mother nature is healing the wounds inflicted by people. When sahib died," Nizmat continued, "the raja declared that he would give us our land back to rent. He felt he had to make at least some profit from it: there was a lot of land but only two families' worth of peasants left. But Tara and I could only take small plots, even though the rent wasn't all that high. If only we could join our properties, and live as one family."

He paused. Ariel was silent too. Sharad was finishing the last rice cake. Lolita watched Ariel from under her eyelashes. He felt her gaze and was moved by it.

CHAPTER FOURTEEN. EVEN GODS CAN BE JEALOUS OF PEOPLE

Ariel and Sharad were resting from their tribulations. Nizmat and Lolita took care of them. They nearly worshipped Ariel. Sharad was already calling Lolita "sister" – "*didi*". He soon recovered his childish exuberance. Nizmat came to love him like a son, "given to us by heaven", and Lolita pampered him as she would a younger brother.

Sharad has found a family.

Ariel pondered Sharad's destiny and his own. He would have felt completely happy among these simple loving people, had they treated him the way they did Sharad. Overbearing reverence that bordered on adoration and religious worship made him feel embarrassed and very awkward. Every morning Lolita brought him wreaths and garlands of flowers, accompanied with respectful bows, as if she was making a sacrifice to a god. He could read in the eyes of the teenage widow as if in an open book – respect mixed with fear was all he could find in her soul. He wished he could see simpler, friendlier feelings in these big dark-brown eyes with long curling black lashes. Ariel tried joking with her, showing her with his entire attitude and behavior that he was just an ordinary man. But Lolita's face remained solemn, stern and respectful, which saddened Ariel.

He went into the woods, made his way deep into the wilderness, stretched on the grass and thought.

How strange and sad his life was! He did not know his parents, had never seen love, friendship or kindness, did not have a real childhood, was not taught anything but a few languages and the drilled-in texts from the sacred books. Then, suddenly, he was made into a flying man. He could fly easier and more freely than a bird! Was it not wonderful? Was it not something people dreamed about? Did they not see themselves flying in their dreams? Weren't these the dreams that brought forth airplanes and dirigibles? Yes, being a flying man would have been really great, had it not separated him from other people. What waited for him at Dandarhat? Piers and Brownlow would have forced him to carry out their will, using him as a hunting hawk, showing him to people as a miracle of nature.

On the other hand, these nice people, Nizmat and Lolita, treated him like a deity. And they weren't the only ones. What about Sharad? Perhaps, all other people would treat him the same way. Did he not possess a trait that had to look superhuman and supernatural to others? Did he have to accept the role of a deity? But that meant sentencing himself to the life of great loneliness and boredom. Lolita, the sweet, gentle half-woman, half-child, would always look up to him, as if he were a creature beyond her reach. Perhaps she liked him, but Lolita would have considered sacrilegious a thought of having a different relationship with him, and insisted on the "divine" patronage on his part and worship on her own.

Besides, he could not stay and live with them. He knew there were people looking for him. He was a rare bird who escaped from his cage. He had to change places, getting further and further away. Unfortunately, his skin was white, albeit tanned by the scorching Indian sun. He was still too pale for an Indian and was bound to attract attention. Coloring his skin with clay was unpleasant and unreliable – the first bit of rain washed it away. Could he find a European suit and pretend to be a sahib? He spoke English very well, but what would he tell people about who he was? He had to consider this. He would not fly. …Except, perhaps, during moonless nights, before dawn, when most people were sound asleep.

He would have to give up Sharad. It was harder to fly with him, and they were more likely to be recognized if they remained together. Sharad was settled. He would be taken care of and pampered like a "gift of the gods", like Nizmat's son sent by heaven.

And what of Lolita? Ariel sighed.

May she find all possible happiness, perhaps even the incredibly rare happiness for an Indian widow – she should marry Ishvar. He was a kind young man and she would be happy with him. Ariel would help them. It was too bad that Ishvar's mother was blind. She would have followed "the will of the gods", had she seen Ariel descending to her from the sky. But the others would tell her, and she would come to believe.

A piercing screech sounded over Ariel's head. He saw two white-bearded monkeys among the thick tree branches. One was large, and the other one was somewhat smaller. The big monkey was trying to take away a piece of fruit from the small one. The small one screeched, while its bigger opponent scratched it, pulled its ears and tail. The smaller monkey cried so pitifully, possibly calling for its mother, that Ariel couldn't stand it and flew up to them.

The monkeys were so struck that they instantly went quiet. But when Ariel reached out to pull them apart, they dashed in the opposite direction, hopping away from one branch to another, from one tree to the next. Once they put enough distance between themselves and Ariel, they both screamed what must have been their alarm, to which other monkeys and birds responded from the different corners of the woods. Ariel smiled sadly, "Even the monkeys are afraid of me," and looked around. A solid canopy of succulent green leaves was above his head. The tree trunks were wound with crawling plants and vines. Here and there, sunbeams penetrated the foliage and made golden spots on the ground, covered in shrubs and grass. This was a wild place. No one saw him. Still, he should not have flown. He couldn't help it.

Maneuvering between the vines, Ariel descended slowly. He heard a rustling. Ariel looked back and saw Ishvar. The young man dropped a bundle of firewood he was carrying and fell to his knees. Ariel landed next to him and said, "Rise, Ishvar, do not be afraid!"

Ishvar slowly got up. His face was pale. His hands were shaking. A god appeared to him and addressed him by name! Gods knew everything.

"Do you love Lolita, Ishvar?"

"My heart is full of her, master, like a goblet filled with rose oil!" Ishvar exclaimed. "If this love is sinful, forgive me. And if you cannot forgive me, take my love away, along with my life!"

"I bless your love, Ishvar," Ariel replied in the same solemn tone of voice. "Go and tell your mother Tara."

"Your words fill my love-sick heart with joy. But may your kindness and mercy fill my soul to the brim. Return eyesight to my mother, so that she could see the gladdened face of her son!"

Ariel was taken aback.

"Everyone has his own karma, Ishvar," he replied and flew away. Ishvar stood there for a long time, looking at the trees that concealed Ariel.

On the same day, Ariel had a long conversation with Nizmat.

At the end of it, Nizmat called his granddaughter and said, "Our great guest, Lolita, blesses your marriage with Ishvar. Tara will agree. She cannot refuse."

Lolita's cheeks flushed, and her eyes shone with joy. She threw herself at Ariel's feet and "accepted dust from his soles". Ariel pulled her up. Her eyes were filled with gratitude!

"Be happy!" he said and smiled. But the god's smile was sad. Even a god could sometimes be jealous of ordinary people!

CHAPTER FIFTEEN. CAN DUST DREAM OF THE SUN?

"Do you love him very much, *didi*?" Sharad asked Lolita.

He was watering flowers in pots arranged along the ledge surrounding the porch. Lolita sat near a small broiler and flipped vegetables simmering in oil with a spatula.

"Who, Sharad?"

"Your groom, Ishvar."

Lolita thought about it and did not say anything.

"Why won't you answer?"

"I don't know, Sharad, whether I love him," she finally replied.

"Then why were you so happy when Ariel said he would help you marry? I saw the way your eyes flashed."

Lolita went silent again. Her hands were shaking.

"You are still a child, Sharad, and it is difficult for you to understand. Ishvar is a good man. And I know he loves me, even though we barely spoke two words to each other."

"Why?"

"Because his mother doesn't allow him to visit us, talk to me, or even look at me, for fear I might defile him. But he still looks and I can see that he loves me, even though he doesn't dare speak of it."

"Is he not a pariah himself?"

"Yes, he is, but his family is a step or two higher than ours. It is very difficult to remain a widow for the rest of your life, Sharad. Grandpa Nizmat is so sad that his family shall fade away. He is growing older. It is very difficult for him to work. And if Nizmat dies, what will happen to me? I shall have no other choice but to drown myself, as many widows do."

Sharad pondered.

"Do you love Ariel?"

"Be quiet Sharad!" Lolita exclaimed in alarm. Blood drained from her cheeks and she frowns. "One mustn't even think of such things!"

"Why?" Sharad refused to give up.

"Can the road dust, trodden by many feet, dream of the sun in the sky?"

"The sun shines both upon a lotus blossom and upon the dust on the road," Sharad said solemnly and then squinted in mischief. "Ariel is not the sun. He is a regular person, like you and me. Except someone taught him how to fly, and I can't."

Nizmat came home. Sharad quietly slipped away and ran into the woods. He wove through bamboo thickets, like a bloodhound, until he found Ariel lying under a tree deep in thought.

"There is something I must tell you, *dada*!" Sharad knelt next to Ariel and told him about his conversation with Lolita.

Dandarhat has taught Ariel to conceal his feelings, but Sharad still noticed that the story had an effect upon his friend.

"And now let's go have breakfast, *dada*. Nizmat is back from the field."

"Let's go, Sharad!" And Ariel playfully ruffled the boy's hair. They went to the cabin.

"The old man works, and Lolita works, and all I do is lie on the grass all day," Ariel said to Sharad. "But what am I to do with them? I have offered them my help many times, and Nizmat won't even listen.

The old man met Ariel as happily and reverently as usually. All Nizmat could think of now was his granddaughter's wedding. As poor as he was, he wanted to have a wedding as nice as any other. He wanted to have wedding flutes, parting songs Bairavi, and a canopy in the yard built from bamboo posts and decorated with garlands of flowers. They could get as many lanterns as they could to replace the expensive candelabras. It would be nice to invite a wind orchestra, but that was too expensive. The flowers could be taken care of by Lolita and Sharad. All they needed to do now was set the date as quickly as possible.

"Perhaps we should wait until pudzhi holiday?" Ariel said.

"Why wait until autumn?" Nizmat objected. "The sooner the better. Have you talked to Tara, master?"

"No. I shall do it tomorrow," Ariel replied. He was very absent-minded, hardly ate anything, and glanced frequently at Lolita, whose eyes were stubbornly fixed on the floor.

After breakfast, Ariel went into the woods once again. In his walks he went further and further away from the cabin.

During one of his forays, he stepped out of the woods and halted, struck by a sudden vision. A large square pond framed with white stone sparkled blindingly before him. On the opposite side were white castles, as huge as mountains, as ornate as jewelry of hammered gold, and as light as lace. The wall of one of the palaces descended into the pond, and it was reflected in its waters with all its beautifully carved galleries, light towers of various heights and shapes, resembling fantastic flowers, its balconies and its fanciful roofs.

In the center of the building a majestic dome converged into a small, thin, carved bell tower. The structure was covered from top to bottom with carvings, arabesques, and seemingly moving fanciful lines. It all looked like a strange dream.

When Ariel told Nizmat about his find, the latter was surprised, "So that's where you went, master! Those are the palaces of our Raja Rajkumar."

Since then, the magical sight attracted Ariel like a magnet. This was the first time he laid eyes on truly beautiful architecture, and it deeply touched his soul.

He often made his way to the hidden palaces and admired them through the branches, as if they were alive. Sometimes he could hear a gentle sound of the gong and human voices.

It was a mysterious world, and one forbidden to him!

After his conversation with Sharad, overwhelmed by his tumultuous thoughts, he walked toward the palaces, without realizing it, as he pushed aside branches and ignored the singing and twittering of birds and squealing calls of monkeys.

"Does she love me? Not Ishvar but me?" Ariel thought, as his heart ached sweetly and his breath caught.

He could stay with these good kindly people, marry Lolita, and work the land. But could the "road dust" rise to the sun? Why couldn't she rise by the power of love? Ishvar would be devastated. But he is already unhappy. Tara did not agree to his marriage before, perhaps she wouldn't agree now, despite Ariel's arguments. Blind people were mistrustful. But what of his accursed gift? His misfortune of being not like the others? Perhaps he could convince Lolita. And Piers? Piers, who wouldn't rest until he caught him and had him chained. Piers, like a sinister shadow, darkened the light of his life. No, dreaming about personal happiness was not for Ariel, destined to eternal exile. He had to go away and leave Lolita. Birdsong sounded like the jingling of bracelet on Lolita's dark wrists and ankles, the dappled sunlight – like her shining eyes, the fragrant breeze – like her breath. Lolita seemed to dissolve in all of nature, surrounded, enshrouded, embraced him, like air. His head was spinning.

CHAPTER SIXTEEN. TRAPPED AGAIN

Without realizing it, Ariel turned, came to the edge of the pond and followed a path toward the palaces, not noticing their dazzling splendor this time.

A hysterical female scream interrupted his thoughts.

Ariel halted and looked around.

To his left was a low stone wall separating the raja's garden from the road. A half-naked dark-skinned man was sweeping the path. There was a well in the garden beyond the wall. A woman in a green silk sari stood near the well. She was leaning over the opening, pulling at her disheveled hair and screaming desperately, "My son! My son! Help! He fell into the well!"

The sweeper threw down his broom, jumped over the wall and ran to the well to rescue the boy.

But when the woman saw him, she blocked his way, like an enraged lioness, her arms spread wide.

"Don't you dare!" she shouted. "Don't come any closer! Your breath is defiling!"

"But you were asking for help," the dismayed sweeper said and stopped.

"I would rather have my sun drown and die than be defiled by your touch!" she exclaimed fanatically.

The half-naked man was a pariah belonging to the line of hereditary sweepers. He lowered his head, like a beaten dog, and stumbled toward the wall, hopped over, and picked up his broom, shaking his head.

And the woman screamed again, "Help! Help!"

Servants ran out from the palace. But they too were all pariahs. Seeing the way the woman attacked the sweeper, the servants halted at the distance established by tradition, not knowing what to do. Some of them ran back to the palace, perhaps realizing that they should call on someone from a higher caste.

The woman grew hoarse and stopped screaming. All she could do now was stare into the well in numb terror. All became eerily silent.

Suddenly Ariel heard faint pitiful crying of a child that sounded like bleating of a baby goat.

Forgetting everything, he soared up, flew in an arch from the road to the well and, slowing down his flight, descended into it. The witnesses shrieked and remained still, while the child's mother fell on the ground by the well.

Cool air surrounded Ariel. The well was deep. Ariel couldn't see anything after the bright sunlight. But soon he saw water shimmering at the bottom, and a dark spot in the middle of it. The child must have been splashing around – there were circles on the water. Something brushed against Ariel's hand. It was a rope.

Once all the way at the bottom, Ariel saw that there was a bucket attached to the rope. It was floating on its side and already half-filled with water. There was a boy of three or four years old in the bucket. With every movement he made the bucket filled up more and more. A minute longer, and the boy would have drowned.

Ariel grabbed the child and started rising slowly. Water streamed from the boy and fell to the bottom. There were large drops of moisture on the moldy stone walls of the well.

Bright light and warmth surrounded Ariel's head and shoulders. He blinked, then squinted, trying to find a good spot to set down the child, then closed his eyes again, flew over the edge of the well and up to the woman. Someone pulled the child from his arms. At the same moment he was grabbed by several pairs of hands.

Ariel opened his eyes wide and saw that he was surrounded by people dressed in rich silk robes, embroidered with gold. A large diamond on someone's crimson tunic flashed in a rainbow of colors.

"Untie the rope from the bucket," the man with the diamond said imperiously.

Several servants rushed to the well, pulled up the bucket and untied the rope.

Ariel was handed over to the servants. They tied him up, while people in silk robes walked away to avoid defiling.

"Take him to the palace!" the man with the diamond commanded.

Before the astonished Ariel could say a single word, he was led to the palace, tied up and surrounded by a crowd of servants, one of whom was holding the end of the rope.

"I can't fly away!" Ariel thought.

He heard the mother of the rescued boy say to an old woman, "Damini! Take Anat and take him to my rooms at the *zenan*[vi]. I cannot touch him. He might be defiled."

CHAPTER SEVENTEEN. THE BONE OF CONTENTION

"When are we going to the sanatorium school, Mister Boden? We have been in Madras for six days, and I still don't know anything about the fate of my brother."

"Patience, Jane," Boden replied, following his steak with a glass of port. He believed that no matter where an Englishman went, he ought to have his favorite dishes and beverages on his table. "I have told you that the school is under quarantine. This damn country is always neck-deep in epidemics. One is constantly at risk of catching malaria or even worse. Sickness is rampant. A valet might set your table with cholera, and a local newsboy might sell you the plague along with the latest newspaper."

"Isn't the plague transmitted through rodents and their fleas?" Jane asked as she pushed away her unfinished fish course, having learned a few things about India from her books.

"The most terrible form of the plague, the lung plague, is transmitted through objects. Don't you know that? That is why I recommended that you stay indoors and do not read papers."

"I am practically in solitary confinement as is," Jane said with a sigh. "I've come all the way to India and seen nothing but these rooftops." Jane waved at the "Black city" – the district where the locals lived beyond the Cooum river.

They sat on the flat roof of an eight-story hotel, equipped with all the European comforts.

The striped orange and yellow awning protected them from the scorching sun. Palms in large tubs and vases with flowers were scattered between the tables. Electric fans hummed on the tables. Silver buckets were stocked with beverages on ice.

The hotel was not far from the river. From the windows of her suite Jane could observe the colorful life of the "Black city". Crowds of dark, chocolate-, and saffron-colored people in colorful costumes moved up and down the narrow winding streets, and Jane, remembering what she read in the books, tried to determine their race. There were donkeys, oxen, and horses, carts creaked, dogs barked. Flutes whistled and drums crackled dully, beggars sang, *saniasi* – the "saints" – recited sacred hymns attracting quite an audience; half-naked children darted here and there with monkey-like agility.

The flat sun-baked roofs were empty. But when the sun went down, the air turned cooler, the sky became dotted with large stars, and the moon rose – the special, Indian moon, flooding the entire world with fantastic greenish light and coal-black shadows – the streets turned empty, but the flat roofs filled with people, coming out to enjoy the fresh evening air. They came out with straw mats, cushions, and platters of food and engaged in lively conversation. From one roof to the next, shrill voices transmitted the latest news about deaths, illnesses, births, weddings, and engagements; about family feuds, purchases and business losses. Through this chaotic telegraph, all of the day's events soon became known to the entire "Black city".

Had Jane known any of the local languages, she would have heard some interesting gossip about the flying man who had been causing quite a stir. But Jane perceived it all as nothing more than "loud gibberish" that irritated her.

Frequently, all too frequently, there were funeral processions in the streets. The shrill sounds of the flutes were gut-wrenching. The bodies were taken outside of the city for the ceremonial burning. Women dressed in white mourning robes wept loudly.

People in the "Black city" died almost as often as they were born.

Jane hurried to step away from the window to avoid seeing this plentiful death crop.

It was no wonder that Boden managed to completely frighten the girl. Since their arrival to Madras, she only visited the botanical garden that struck her with its splendid variety of tropical plants. On the way back she got to see an elephant, covered with a blanket and with a guide on its back.

"Perhaps it's an elephant from a circus?" the girl thought.

"Dotaller keeps disappearing somewhere," she said, absent-mindedly peeling a banana. She hardly ate anything but bananas and hard-boiled eggs, considering them to be the best protected from infection.

"Mister Dotaller, like me, doesn't like to be idle for long," Boden objected, having transitioned to his favorite cocktails and liqueurs. "We are hoping to have some good news for you soon."

Boden and Dotaller really were busy. At least, their minds were most actively engaged.

During their trip they treated each other as enemies, and each tried to learn the character and weaknesses of the other. Their goals contradicted: Boden would have preferred if Aurelius went mad but lived as long as possible; whereas Dotaller would have been happier in the case of Aurelius' death, for all of his estate would then go to Jane. Dotaller had the power of attorney from Jane for conducting all her financial affairs. Using her inexperience, he could transition her capital into his own pockets without any trouble.

Boden spent a lot of time thinking. He did not have the owl-like eyes of his partner to consult along the way, and this made him less decisive.

What to do? Tell Jane about Dotaller's behavior or join forces with him?

The problem was that Jane mistrusted Boden and Heslon so strongly that even if she had an argument with Dotaller, she still wouldn't trust the honored partners with her estate. But how was he to engage Dotaller? Create a Boden-Heslon-Dotaller union and split the profits three ways? But Aurelius' estate was far greater than that of his sister. The triple split was not at all advantageous for Boden and Heslon. He had to come up with another idea. Oh, how Boden missed the perceptive eyes of his partner!

Still, Boden started preparing the foundation for a possible agreement. Dotaller acted evasively. Once in Madras, he pursued his own line of investigation.

Piers, with whom Boden met every day without Jane's knowledge, once told Boden that Dotaller had already hinted to him (Piers) that if Aurelius was found dead or found and *made* dead, then Piers would receive a large compensation. Piers, the scoundrel that he was, took the opportunity to suggest to Boden that whether Ariel would live or die depended on who would pay him more – Boden or Dotaller.

"First of all, we must find Ariel," Boden said to Piers.

"And what do you intend to do with him then?" Piers asked.

"Have him declared mentally incompetent through courts and keep him in London under lock and key. Don't forget that I am his legal guardian!" Boden replied irritably.

The two-faced Janus, Piers-Bharava, did not like that answer. A flying man was the most valuable asset of the Theosophical Society and, therefore, to Piers himself. Losing him or killing him was highly unprofitable. But it would be better to kill him than to let go of him entirely.

Piers didn't say that to Boden, but decided that, when the time came, it would be better to accept Boden's offer. Let Boden obtain the lifelong guardianship of Ariel and manage his estate, while Ariel would be presented to the theosophists for a large sum – the London headquarters was bound to agree.

But first of all, Ariel had to be located. Piers knew that Ariel and Sharad traveled on the wing of an airplane headed for Madras and left it not far from the city. After that, their tracks vanished.

"In any case, they should be somewhere in the vicinity of Madras," Piers said. "Hunger will force them to seek out people. My agents have been dispatched to all the villages."

"But Ariel can fly away from them," Boden objected.

"With Sharad, he won't get very far and he will not leave him behind either," Piers stated with certainty.

Neither of them knew that Ariel and Sharad took another plane flying in the opposite direction to Bengali.

"One last question," Boden said. "You, Piers, must have a talk with Miss Galton. After all, I cannot just take her to a non-existent sanatorium school. You must portray the headmaster of this mythical sanatorium." And Boden explained to Piers how to behave and what to discuss with Jane.

The meeting between Piers and Jane Galton took place on the same day.

In a European suit and large tortoise shell glasses Piers looked very imposing and trustworthy.

He apologize for not being able to visit her earlier. The school was under quarantine. Piers expressed his regrets regarding the sad fate of her mentally ill brother. The school was doing everything possible to restore Aurelius' mental health, he was being treated by the best psychiatrists, but the illness turned out to be too complex. During one of his lapses Aurelius escaped, despite being carefully watched. Many mental patients possessed great cunning, courage and resourcefulness. He snuck up to one of the roofs, jumped from the roof to the tree and ran away. But she need not worry. He would be apprehended. All measures had been taken.

Jane wanted to ask Piers in detail about the nature of Ariel's illness, but just then, Dotaller joined them unexpectedly. He had been gone three days. He looked tired and anxious. He did not even shave or change out of his traveling suit.

"Aurelius has been located!" he exclaimed without greeting anyone and fell into an armchair.

"Where? How?" Questions followed.

"I am deathly tired. Give me something to drink, please!"

Jane gave him a glass of water.

"Thank you. Here is how I found him: as soon as we came to Madras, I reached out to a colleague of mine, Walton, the lawyer, who has been living in India for the last twenty years and knows it like the back of his hand. He has tremendous connections. I asked him to let me know immediately, if he finds out anything new about the flying man."

"The flying man?" Jane asked in astonishment.

"Yes, about Aurelius. It's his obsession, weren't you told? He imagines that he can fly. And so, three days ago Mister Walton called me and informed me that he had a client in Udaipur. The client heard from a friend who had recently visited a local raja, that the raja had acquired a flying man. There were no other details, but at least I had one end of the thread in my hands."

"Why didn't you tell us about this?" Boden asked with displeasure.

"I could not waste a single minute, you understand," Dotaller said angrily.

"You should have sent a telegraph. We would have helped," Boden was becoming anxious. But Dotaller ignored his statement and continued, "I went to the airport directly after visiting Walton and flew to Calcutta, and then to Udaipur, where I found Walton's friend and found out where the raja's residence was located, after which I went to visit him. Raja Rajkumar was described to me as a typical despot and petty tyrant. He refused to see me. Then I managed to bribe some of the servants who told me that the flying man really was at the raja's palace. They did not say how he got there. But they did tell me that the flying man was a source of great amusement to the raja. Having discovered all this, I immediately set out on the return trip and, as you can see, came to see you right away to tell you about my find. How can you reproach me, Mister Boden?"

"You only came back because the raja refused to see you and you needed our help," Boden noted acidly.

"Even so, what is wrong with that?" Dotaller objected. "Had the raja agreed to receive me and given me Aurelius, we would have returned together, that is all."

Boden did not consider it necessary to continue arguing with Dotaller. But it was clear to both Boden and Piers that Dotaller attempted to control all aspects and, fortunately for them, failed.

Dotaller, however, was far from telling them everything he saw, did and found out.

He really did manage to discover where Aurelius was. He also found out, under which circumstances Aurelius ended up at the raja's palace, although he did not believe that he could fly. The cunning lawyer did not even try meeting with the raja. He had a different goal. Dotaller approached the raja's servants belonging to the lowest and most despised castes. The lawyer was hoping to find suitable material to serve his purposes. He wanted to bribe the servants to kill Aurelius. But the servants turned out to be so intimidated by the raja, that the sahib's suggestion horrified them. They knew that the sahib would be beyond suspicion, while they themselves would be subject to terrible torture if the raja found out about their betrayal.

"Even if you offered me a gold nugget the size of this palace with its tip brushing the sky, I still wouldn't agree," the gray-bearded old gardener told Dotaller. The other servants replied in a similar way.

Dotaller realized that he could not make a deal with these people. Even worse, they could inform the raja about the sahib's plans. It was dangerous to stay on the raja's lands under these circumstances.

Dotaller would not have had any problem arranging a meeting with the raja. Like all local princes, he enjoyed receiving sahibs. But would the raja release Aurelius? That was the question. All the servants said that the raja valued the flying man very highly. And if the raja did let him go, how would it benefit Dotaller?

Having freed Aurelius, Dotaller couldn't very well kill him on his own. The lawyer was too careful to become a direct participant in a murder. However, if Aurelius perished while still at the raja's palace, no one would suspect Dotaller. Of course, Aurelius could also "disappear" after the raja handed him over to Dotaller. He could later say that Aurelius escaped and perished while on the run. But there was a reason Dotaller was a lawyer. He knew from his practice as a defense attorney, that the smallest misstep and lack of planning could lead the criminal to fateful consequences. He also knew that some crimes, seemingly forgotten, sometimes came to light years later. No, it was not his business as a gentleman to soil his hands in blood. Let someone else do it, guided by a skilled hand!

After all, he could also live with the fact of Aurelius remaining alive. The main thing was to get him away from Boden and Piers. Aurelius would soon come of age. Using Jane, Dotaller could take measures to ensure that the courts would declare Aurelius perfectly normal. The guardianship would become defunct. The young man would move in with Jane and, of course, like his sister, give him, Dotaller, the power of attorney over his estate.

Dotaller made a new plan. If Aurelius' sister, his guardian and Dotaller himself went to the raja and stated their rights to see Aurelius, mentioning that Aurelius was the son of a lord and a prosperous businessman, the raja would be forced to concede. Jane would not want to part from her brother. All would be well.

"As I said," Dotaller continued after a general pause, "the raja is a despot and a tyrant. But, if you, Miss Jane, and you, Mister Boden, went to see him…"

"Just as I said," Boden couldn't resist. "You couldn't do without us!"

"I completely agree. Are you trying to start an argument, Mister Boden?"

"I must join you as well," Piers stated.

"Your presence does not appear entirely necessary to me," Dotaller objected, wincing.

"It is extremely necessary," Piers insisted. "As the headmaster of the sanatorium school where Aurelius Galton was being treated, I can testify before the raja that the young man is mentally unstable and, therefore, must be kept under special conditions."

Boden, having evaluated the situation and realized that Dotaller, at present, was his most dangerous opponent, decided to keep an ally on hand and supported Piers. Jane did not object, and Dotaller was forced to agree.

They decided to fly out on the same day.

Dotaller took upon himself the role of a guide. They reached the raja's fantastic palaces without any trouble.

CHAPTER EIGHTEEN. UNSUCCESFUL SEARCH

Jane finally got to see the real India. Despite her anxiety about the upcoming meeting with her sick brother, whom she hadn't seen in many years, the girl was captivated by the beauty of the palaces and gardens. As if on purpose, several elephants paraded past the main entrance just as the car approached. The animals were covered in richly embroidered blankets and were certainly not from a circus.

The raja received the guests very courteously, in a study furnished in the European fashion and wearing a European suit, much to Jane's disappointment.

She wondered how they were going to communicate with the raja. But it turned out that the raja spoke excellent English. Still, he was a typical man of the East. The snow-white front of his starched shirt only emphasized the darkness of his skin. The raja's face made Jane think of Othello.

Boden briefly explained the purpose of their visit.

As he spoke, the raja's face expressed increasing dismay.

"I am very sorry," he said, when Boden finished his speech, "that I cannot satisfy your request: Aurelius Galton, as you call this wondrous young man, really did stay with me, but he is no longer here. And I... I cannot add anything to it. Your Aurelius is gone."

Everyone was stunned by this unexpected news. Jane, Boden, Piers, and Dotaller showered the raja with questions, but the latter only tugged nervously at his curly beard and repeated the same thing, "I cannot add anything to what I've already said. The servants told me that the young man vanished last night, and I haven't heard anything beyond that. Would you like some tea? You must be tired from your trip. No? Perhaps, you would like to see my diamonds?"

"Sir!" Boden exclaimed. "I trust you realize the full responsibility..."

He didn't finish. The mask of false European politeness instantly vanished from the raja's face. His eyes flashed, causing Boden to choke and grow pale.

"I trust that you too take full responsibility for your words, sir!" he interrupted Boden. "I would consider highly offensive a mere thought that I," he made an impact on the word "I", "am saying something that does not entirely correspond to the truth."

Everyone realized that the conversation was over and they would not get anything more out of the raja. Their parting was much cooler and more strained than their initial meeting.

As they descended the marble staircase swathed in carpets and flowers, Boden said quietly to Jane, trying to console her and himself, "Don't worry, Jane, Aurelius must have escaped again. Of course, it is regrettable, but we should be able to find him any day. He couldn't have flo... gone far."

Jane only sighed.

"The raja doesn't want to give up the flying man. He is probably hiding him somewhere," Piers said to Dotaller, as they walked through the park along a low stone wall. "But we'll engage all of our resources, we shall go to the viceroy if we have to and demand a search at the palace and Aurelius' surrender."

Dotaller was thinking something known only to him. Piers walked silently ahead.

Suddenly, Piers heard a voice from beyond the wall. A few words, said in Hindustani, made him halt and listen to the conversation.

A sweeper stood in the middle of the street, and next to him – a thin old man and a teenage girl.

"May I be reborn as the vilest snake if I am lying!" the sweeper said, clearly outraged by their mistrust. "I have spoken to the man who himself, with his own hands, tied up the flying man before he was thrown into a bottomless well on the raja's orders."

The old man gestured the sweeper away, his face wrinkled painfully, and he said dully, "It's all over. Come, Lolita!"

But the girl did not move. She gazed at the old man with half-mad eyes and then said firmly, "He cannot die! He said, 'Wait for me, Lolita,' and I shall wait for him."

"What is it, Mister Piers!" Dotaller exclaimed, catching up to him. He took one glance at Piers' pale face and said anxiously, lowering his voice, "What is the matter?"

"Nothing, nothing… a brief heart episode. It happens… It shall pass."

Dotaller looked at him doubtfully.

In the evening, when they were told that the car was waiting outside to take them out to dinner, Piers decided there was no need to keep the secret any longer. He said to Boden,

"Mister Boden! We have nothing more to argue about. Ariel-Aurelius Galton is dead. He has been killed on the raja's orders."

And Piers told him about the conversation he had overheard.

A loud scream sounded beyond the wall. Oh, those traitorously thin walls of the provincial Indian hotels!

Piers and Boden found Jane in tears.

Dotaller ran in to find out what the noise was all about. Having discovered the reason, he barely contained his joy. Everything was turning out the best possible way for him!

CHAPTER NINETEEN. THE MASTER IS DISPLEASED

The little boy, Anat, rescued by Ariel from the well was the son of the man with the big diamond. The man's name was Mohita, and he was the raja's chief advisor and favorite.

It was very advantageous to be the raja's favorite. Raja Rajkumar possessed treasures, whose value he himself did not know clearly. Few Europeans knew that some of the Indian rajas were the wealthiest people in the world, compared to whom the famous billionaires – the Rothchilds, the Morgans, the Rockefellers, and the Vanderbilts – were comparatively poor people. For centuries, from one generation to the next, the rajas increased their riches, comprising primarily precious stones and gold. Little was known about these treasures, because the rajas felt no need to sell their diamonds, and even if they did, it was not always possible: there were few buyers in the world who could afford The Great Mogol or the Pitt-Regent. Their real estate – palaces and lands – were also vast. But their value did not come close to the piles of rubies and diamonds.

It was no wonder that the rajas could reward their favorites far greater than any of the mightiest and wealthiest European monarchs. However, the raja's kindness and love had to be earned by service. Like all people, leading an idle life in a secluded world, as Voltaire said "in the world without horizons", the raja was most afraid of boredom, even though he was well educated and spoke excellent English. His wife,

Shiama, spoke French like a Parisian. The raja visited Europe with her several times – London, Paris, and Berlin. But tuxedos and smoking jackets, theaters and assemblies, European kitchen and the entire way of life felt restrictive to him compared to his usual loose and light ethnic garb and carefree existence. The entertainments felt alien. And he rushed his wife to go home.

At home, having carried out the purification ritual and shed the restrictive clothing, Rajkumar sighed in relief and felt happy. He spent hours on a couch, dressed in a light silk robe. A servant boy fanned him with a fan made of palm leaves. The raja picked up the books and magazines bought in Europe, chose a "light" novel and read.

One could maintain European habits without going to Europe!

He was a kind of "enlightened absolutist". He belonged to the religious society Brahmo-Samadge, did not worship idols, did not follow the burdensome religious rituals too closely, ate meat prepared by his Muslim chef, followed new publications, read books on philosophy, agreed both with Rousseau and with Nietzsche, enjoyed the company of the sahibs, and was friends with many of them.

Having lounged two or three days with the new book, he suddenly felt that the snake of boredom once again crept into his heart.

And that was when Mohita appeared, having learned the moods of his master to the finest detail.

"What news, Mohita?" the raja asked, carelessly tossing the book onto the carpet.

Mohita "accepted dust" from his master's feet, greeted him formally, and provided a brief report about the household matters, about the new agreements with the sahibs and the peasants, about the rent payments, about the punishment to the delinquent payees.

Presently, the raja listened to him distractedly and interrupted, repeating the question, "What news have you got, Mohita?"

"A group of boys and girls has prepared new dances."

Raja remembered Parisian cancan and chuckled, "It's old. Although, go ahead and show me."

Mohita clapped his hands, the velvet curtains hanging from a tall arch by the door slid open and a group of children ran into the room: girls wrapped in light chiffon with ringing bracelets on their wrists and ankles, and boys in colorful costumes. They started dancing, accompanied by flutes. Their movements were graceful, smiles were frozen on their frightened faces.

"It's old," the raja repeated and waved them away.

The flutes went silent, and the children stopped dancing, huddling together like a frightened flock of sheep. The raja started telling Mohita about the cancan, the women's costumes and their high kicks, "See, their legs went over their heads, and all the ruffles – whoosh!" and he ordered to make such costumes for the girls, with full skirts and high heels, and teach them the cancan. A puzzled Mohita bowed.

"What else have you got?"

"The dance of hunchbacks, cripples and blind men."

This was new.

"Show me."

The children ran out, not hiding their joy that all went well, and no one was to be flogged or imprisoned in the dungeon, which happened often.

Drums rumbled and a strange-looking crowd ran into the room, limping, falling, stumbling, and gasping. They were dressed in costumes made of various colorful patches. Mohita wasted no time during his master's absence. Where did he manage to find these freaks? The hunchbacks with big heads and frog-like mouths, attacked the cripples, knocked them down with their humps, and fell down themselves. The blind men ran their heads together and squealed to the thundering of the drums.

The raja laughed out loud. Mohita beamed.

"Call Rajina Shiama!" the raja exclaimed.

The rajina showed up in a fashionable Parisian dress and shoes with very high heels.

She looked at the dancers and shouted in delight, "How charming!" then sat down on the floor, wrapped her arms around her knees and laughed so hard that her hair came undone.

The raja took off a ring with an enormous diamond and threw it to Mohita, who caught the sparkling gift and bowed.

One of the blind men knocked down by a hunchback fell on his face. Having hit his head on a pillar, he screamed, "I wish you'd die, you damned torturers!"

The raja's face darkened, as did Mohita's. When the cloud fell over the face of the sun, it cast shadows on the ground below.

"He did not mean you, Master, but the hunchbacks!" Mohita rushed to say.

But the raja turned away and mumbled angrily, "A hundred lashes! Leave me."

Everyone left. Mohita was glad that he at least managed to get the ring. But the master was now angry. Mohita ordered the servants to add a hundred lashes from himself. That would be plenty to free the unfortunate man from any more troubles.

Mohita was irked. He had a few more things prepared for the raja. For instance, there were the naked slaves armed with iron sticks with curved claws on the end. The raja was particularly fond of that entertainment. When the slaves wounded each other and blood flowed over their dark bodies, the Rousseau scholar was swept away by the battle spirit, his eyes flashed, and his nostrils flared.

"Get him! Scratch! Harder! Yes! Yes!" he urged his gladiators and was very disappointed when one of them fell to the ground dead and the game ended.

There was also the tiger hunt with a specially prepared splendid elephant with enormous tusks, capped with sharp copper spikes.

But the raja no longer asked for Mohita that day, and the latter was at a loss as to how to recover the master's benefaction.

That was when the incident with his son happened. When the servants told Mohita that his son fell into the well, he ran out and saw Ariel fly in from the street, drop into the well and rescue the boy.

Mohita was not worried about his son. This was the child of his first wife, whom he no longer loved. Besides, he had two other wives.

However, Mohita was struck by the flying man.

He did not ponder what the flying man was – whether he was a supernatural being or a product of some new trick. The most important thing was that this was a completely unusual, new spectacle, a new entertainment. No matter who he was, Mohita could safely show him before the master's angry eyes. Seeing this miracle, the raja would forget about everything, and Mohita would recover his good graces.

And so, Mohita ordered to tie up the flying man, regardless of whether he was another incarnation of Krishna himself.

CHAPTER TWENTY. PEACE IS RESTORED

Mohita led Ariel, tied up and surrounded by servants, into the palace, following the back way past the kitchens teeming with black, chocolate- and saffron-colored half-naked cooks in white hats. They ascended a narrow staircase to the second floor, passed the *zenan*, where children played and wrestled under the supervision of servants. In one room, an elderly woman looked up at Ariel through her glasses, one side held up to her ear with a bit of red twine. The floor of another room was covered with blue and white mats and carpets, with colorful silk cushions scattered here and there. A girl sat on a low couch. Her head was covered with a blue scarf and her shoulders were shaking.

Tears fell from her eyes. An old man stood before the girl, his forehead marked with the sign of his caste painted with red and yellow clay. He was reproaching the girl sternly. Perhaps, she was a prisoner too, just like Ariel.

They followed the gallery with light, filigree columns framing the view of a mirror-calm lake to the raja's half of the palace. The enormous halls with their ceilings covered with sculpted ornaments, with columns and niches painted with arabesques, fantastic flowers, animals, and birds, followed one another as if in a magical kaleidoscope. Sometimes Ariel felt as if he was in a dream. The scent of attar was everywhere – a fragrant oil mixed with the essence of the Dalmatian rose and blossoming oleanders in large vases covered with glossy colorful glazes. Ariel's head spun from the fragrances and sights.

"Wait here," Mohita ordered the servants guarding Ariel when they came up to a crimson drape suspended from golden curtain rings.

Someone's angry voice could be heard from beyond the drape. One of the servants tugged the end of the rope wrapped around Ariel's hands, and Ariel stopped.

Mohita anxiously slipped behind the drape.

Bowing to the ground, he approached the raja, whose face was becoming increasingly angry. Mohita saw nothing but that face.

"I did not ask for you Mohita! Why are you here?" the raja asked sternly.

Mohita continued bowing humbly and nearly writhing with his entire body, as he approached the raja and whispered something into his ear. Expressions of surprise, doubt, curiosity, once again surprise, and once again doubt followed each other on the raja's face.

Mohita anxiously watched these changes.

"I hope he doesn't kick me out!" Mohita thought.

"Very well. Show him to me. But if you are deceiving me, remember: your wives will wear the widows' white by sundown!"

Mohita ran behind the drape and ordered to bring Ariel in.

Ariel entered the hall and was dazzled and blinded on the spot. Bright sunrays fell from somewhere above, shone on gilded walls and pillars and sparkled over precious stones decorating people's clothes, as they crowded by delicate spiraling columns. An enormous golden nugget lay on raspberry carpets and cushions under a dark-blue canopy and shimmered with all colors of the rainbow.

Having recovered, Ariel saw that what he mistook for a gold nugget was the raja himself, dressed in a gold-embroidered robe. Diamonds scattered over his clothes had to be worth millions, and his turban was decorated with such an enormous gem that one could not imagine its value.

The raja was dark-skinned, with a somewhat flat nose and full, almost Negroid lips, despite his family tree records, ascertaining that he was a pure-blooded Hindu.

The raja leveled his bright black eyes at Ariel. Only the Dandarhat training enabled Ariel to withstand his gaze.

Then the raja glanced at his court, dressed more garishly than the peacocks and parrots in his gardens.

The raja ordered Ariel to come closer.

The servants nudged Ariel forward.

"Who are you?" the raja asked.

Ariel was still deciding how to act and said nothing.

"Who are you?" the raja repeated in English, thinking that Ariel did not know Hindustani.

The youth remained silent.

Mohita asked the same question in Bengali and Marathi, then switched to the Dravidian languages Telugu and Tamil, and then, finally, to Tibetan and Birman tongues with the same result.

The raja frowned and said, "He is either deaf or stubborn. But I shall force him to speak!" and his eyes flashed. "Can you fly?" the raja asked, switching back to Hindustani.

Mohita couldn't stand it and, coming closer to Ariel, smacked him upside the head and said, "Speak, you idiot, if you don't want to lose your tongue altogether!"

Ariel's lips moved, but he said nothing. He decided that if he pretended to be deaf and did not show his ability to fly, perhaps they would let him go.

The raja snatched the fan from his servant and threw it at Mohita, stomping his feet, "Scoundrel! You brought me some kind of an idiots!"

"Have mercy, oh master of my life!" Mohita exclaimed, falling to his knees before the raja. "I did not lie! Ask them," he pointed at the servant, "ask my wife Bintiaba-sini. Everyone saw this man, or spirit in human form, fly! Order him whipped, and he shall speak and fly!"

"He will get his share of lashing, but you won't escape yours either!" and the raja clapped his hands.

The curtains to the right from the throne opened. An enormous curly-haired man appeared by the raja's side. He was as black as ebony wood and carried a cat-o-nine-tails, always ready to obey his master.

The raja silently pointed at Mohita. The executioner raised his whip and brought it down with a whistle. Mohita was huddled on the floor, screaming at the top of his lungs and curling into a ball.

Ariel straightened out and suddenly said, "Stop it! Yes, I can fly!"

The whip froze in the air, and the raja fell back against the cushions in astonishment, then yelled at the servants, "Hold on to that rope! If he flies away, I shall take your heads off!"

Ariel knelt. Mohita kept gasping, but his face shone. The storm was over! He propped himself up and sat on the floor.

"Who are you?" the raja asked again, looking at Ariel with some fear. More than anything else, Ariel was afraid that they would send him back to Dandarhat, and so he said, "I do not know who I am and where I am from."

The raja was puzzled.

"What do you mean you don't know? You flew into my park from the street. Where were you before that?"

"I know no more than a newborn baby. I gained my senses in the street," Ariel said the first thing that popped into his head.

"Then how do you know about newborn babies?" the raja asked.

Ariel was taken aback, not knowing what to say.

"I think you are a little confused," the raja said. But there was no more anger in his voice.

His imagination was deeply struck by the flying man.

He had to be careful with this youth. What an acquisition! Neither pharaohs nor the greatest emperors had such a toy! If only he could tame this human bird!

"What is your name?"

Ariel thought about it and replied, "Siddha."

It was a name of one of the spirits from Indian mythology.

"Siddha? Very well, let it be Siddha," the raja said after a pause.

"Oh, merciful Master!" Mohita reminded of himself, having recovered.

The raja glanced at him benevolently and said, "The treasurer shall give you a cror[vii] of rupees. And nine hundred sacks of rupees for the nine scars you have received."

Mohita bowed to the ground. Of course, the raja would not give him quite that much gold, but he would not leave him entirely without reward.

"Listen, Siddha, stay with me and you won't regret it."

Rajina Shiama entered.

She was dressed in a sari. A golden tiara of magnificent workmanship decorated her forehead and was held to her black hair by pins with large emeralds and blood-colored rubies. A massive necklace of hammered gold circled her neck, and rows of platinum bangles jingled around her ankles. Her sari was bright-green, in accordance with her faith, and her arms were covered with bracelets from shoulders to wrist, including those made of gold and the more fragile glass ones, held up with silk ties. Among all these locally-made jewelry pieces, the rajina wore several gold bracelets with precious stones made by the best Parisian jewelers.

It was difficult to imagine, by looking at her, that this woman that looked like a fairy-tale queen, also knew how to wear European dresses and high-heeled shoes.

"Listen, Shiama..." the raja said. "Mohita found me a new wonder."

At these words, the faithful servant and confidant started smiling and bowing. The raja was in a good mood and wanted to cover for his earlier outburst by praising Mohita in front of his wife.

"Look, this young man can fly," he continued, pointing at Ariel with his bejeweled finger.

"So that's who he is! I have already heard that he rescued Anat. He must be rewarded for it," Shiama said, approaching Ariel. "Why is he tied up? Poor lad! And so handsome! Untie his hands!" she ordered the servants.

"Untie his hands, but wrap a rope around his waist," the raja hurried to add, fidgeting restlessly on his cushions. "And hold it tight! And now, Siddha, show us what you can do."

Ariel rose into the air. The servant gradually paid out the rope, as if for an aerostat. Ariel flew up to the high ceiling and started circling and looking at the sculpted ornaments.

The raja watched him with interest and anxiety, leaning back on the cushions.

Shiama stepped away to have a better view and watched the flying man, her face pale with wonder.

"Astonishing!" she exclaimed.

"That's enough, Siddha! Come down."

Ariel did.

"What does it mean?" Shiama asked, greatly moved. "Who is he? A god? A man?"

"Siddha doesn't want to tell us about it," the raja replied. "But he will. And he will stay with us. Won't you, Siddha? You won't fly away from us, will you? Whether you are a god or a man, you won't have a better life in heaven or on earth than you can have here. Will you stay?"

"I will."

"Splendid. Don't be offended, but will keep an eye on you."

"Perhaps, you are hungry, Siddha?" Shiama asked gently.

Ariel looked at her with gratitude. Only a woman would have thought to ask him.

But Ariel was a little mistaken: Shiama was a kind woman, but she had another thought, when she asked the question, "Gods do not need food." She expected Siddha to reveal his true nature by his answer – whether he was a god or a man.

"Yes, I am hungry," Ariel answered simply and with a smile.

"Not a god!" Shiama thought.

In the meantime, the raja quietly gave Mohita the most strict and precise directions as to how to protect and provide for Siddha.

In conclusion, the raja took two rings off his finger and threw them to Mohita. Peace between them was restored.

CHAPTER TWENTY-ONE. AGREED

Ariel was taken to a room adjacent to the raja's bedroom. The raja wanted to have Siddha nearby.

Twelve servants were assigned to the flying creature, as if he was a prince. Although, the servants were also the captive's guards.

With deep bows, they offered Master Siddha to take a bath with fragrant oils, then dressed him in expensive clothes and brought him a delicious and plentiful dinner.

The fruit platter included some rare pieces, including the Burman mangosteens, which Ariel had never seen before and did not know how to eat them. He squeezed and pinched the fruit awkwardly and tried to bite it.

A respectable old Hindu serving him said as imperiously as a Brahmin, hiding a smile in his moustache, "Cut it in half with the knife, Master, and taste what's inside."

"He doesn't know all that much for a god," the old man thought to himself.

After dinner Ariel happily stretched out on a couch. A dark-skinned boy stood over him with a fan. Swallows dashed by the tall grated window and Ariel envied them.

This was better than Dandarhat, but still, he could not be at rest. He already had a certain impression of the raja, who went so easily from kindness to cruelty. Ariel was well at the moment, but what would happen tomorrow? With what pleasure he would trade this gilded cage for Nizmat's modest cabin! What would the old man, Lolita, and Sharad think of him? He disappeared so suddenly... Was he destined to go from one cage to the next for the rest of his life? Why could he not be as free as the swallows? Had it not been for the grate on the window, Ariel would have flown away with them into the blue vastness of the sky.

Through the course of the day, the raja looked in on Ariel several times and asked whether he was comfortable and whether he was happy with the food and the servants.

The raja couldn't wait to play with his new toy, but Shiama convinced him not to bother Siddha – let him rest for a day. The raja, despite his propensity for Eastern despotism, often yielded to his favorite rajina, who was one of the most beautiful and intelligent women in India and his trusted assistant in dealings with the sahibs. What he could not get from them, Shiama achieved with a few clever words and a charming smile.

Several times, when Ariel woke up during the night, he saw the raja standing over him in a robe and pointy shoes.

In the morning, the door opened, and the raja entered, carrying a stack of newspapers. He sat down next to Ariel and said, "We have found out a little about you, Siddha! I don't like reading newspapers, but my secretary pointed out this article about a flying man. Of course, it is about you. And, of course, you did not just appear in this world yesterday, in the middle of the road before my palace. Listen, Siddha, no matter who you are," the raja cooed as kindly and gently as a dove, "trust me, and you won't lose. Come, I want to show you something. But I have already warned you. Don't be offended: until we have reached an agreement and become friends, I shall keep you on a chain. My blacksmiths and jewelers worked all night and made a golden chain for you. But it was a bit too heavy and not quite strong enough. So, we made you another one – a steel one, with a golden belt. Paresh!" the raja shouted.

A servant entered, placed the golden circlet around Ariel's waist, locked it, and handed the key and the end of the chain to the raja.

"Come!" the raja repeated, firmly holding the chain.

He led Ariel down the endless enfilade of halls, decorated with gold, marble, ivory, and majolica. Mosaic, sculptures, jewels, figurines, and flowers were everywhere.

The walls of one hall were covered entirely with amber, the second one – with crystal, the third – with tiles of ivory. A pair of enormous elephant tusks decorated with the finest carving hung over the door in a golden frame.

From the "elephant hall", a staircase led downward.

They descended for a long time, until they came into the cellar. The raja picked up a lantern and followed a corridor. There was another staircase leading to an even deeper cellar, and finally they stopped before a cast-iron door with bas-reliefs portraying fantastic snakes and dragons.

"We are now under the lake you saw from your window," the raja said and opened the heavy door. "Come on."

"Does the raja want to lock me in the dungeon?" Ariel thought, entering the dark room.

Something clicked, and the space was flooded with dazzling lights.

The walls of the low vault were lined with trunks fettered with copper. Their lids suddenly popped open, and Ariel's astonished eyes were presented with a sight one rarely got to see. Some of the boxes seemed to be filled with blood – they were overflowing with large rubies. The others appeared to contain sea water – the emeralds. Yet others shimmered with the diamond rainbow. There were trunks with topazes, chrysolites, pearls, turquoise, rubies, agates, sapphires, garnets, chrysoprases, aquamarines, tourmalines. Red, blue, black, green, and yellow jewels were everywhere – some sparkling, some matte and subdued.

Beyond them were trunks with gold ingots and golden sand, with silver, and with platinum.

It seemed incredible that so many treasures were assembled in one palace, in possession of one man.

"Do you understand, Siddha, the meaning of these pretty little stones and gold? This is power over people. One stone – and any sahib official will do anything I want. I have given them many stones. A slightly larger stone – and the viceroy follows my every wish. A yet larger stone – and the King of England himself bestows the title of a lord upon me and sends me courteous letters. I will show them to you. And so, Siddha, no matter who you are, no matter what your past, I can help you stay here, if that is what you wish. Here, you will get something that you will not find anywhere else. Think about it. You need not answer now. I shall visit with you after breakfast."

They returned to the palace.

Ariel was left alone. More than anything else, he feared ending up in Piers' hands again. No one but the raja could possibly protect Ariel, if Piers ever found him. Ariel had no doubt about it. At the moment, the raja was benevolent. Why not trust him? Lolita was nearby, he would manage to see her. "But if the raja's mercy turns to rage..." Ariel smile and flew up to the ceiling. "Won't I be able to fly away?"

When the raja came back after breakfast, Ariel told him honestly everything he knew about himself and about the Dandarhat school.

The raja was very interested in his story, particularly in the school.

"Are there any other miraculous young men, such as yourself?" he asked.

"There are those, whose body glows or emits a fragrance, there are mind readers and seers."

"I should tell Mohita about it. But you, young man, are a miracle of miracles. Well then, do you agree to stay with me of your own free will? If the answer is yes, then I shall remove the grate from the window and throw your chain away into the pond."

"And if I don't agree, you will throw me into the pond instead of the chain," Ariel thought and replied, "I agree. But who are you and what is your name?"

The raja laughed.

"You must have really fallen from the sky. I am Raja Rajkumar. You may simply call me Rajkumar. You are an unusual man after all, even though you are only a man. I am very glad, Ariel. From now on, you have complete freedom within the boundaries of my palaces and parks. But no further! Do you promise?"

Ariel thought about Lolita – he did not tell the raja about her – and wanted to ask permission to fly around the vicinity, but decided that it was too early for such a request and replied, "I promise."

The raja was extremely pleased. With the flying man not limited by the chain, he could come up with many more amusements. That was the most important thing.

On the same day, the grate was taken down from the window, and the chain was thrown into the pond.

CHAPTER TWENTY-TWO. THE NEW TOY

One would think that the raja, who was fond of all manner of novelties, became obsessed with Siddha-Ariel. He not only abandoned all business, but all of his favorite amusements, including the gladiator battles and hunting. He was with Ariel from morning until night, making him do all kinds of tricks and coming up with the new ones. Ariel obeyed the raja willingly, and sometimes even happily.

Having gathered his entire household into the largest and highest hall, the raja sprawled on the cushions and commanded, "Rise to the ceiling, Ariel! Fly in circles! Standing! Lying down! Faster! Faster! Tumble! Come here, Ariel! Take the monkey and fly with it!"

Ariel grabbed the monkey and rose. The monkey screeched and tried to pull out from his hands. The spectators laughed until they cried, and the raja laughed most of all. The monkey scratched Ariel, finally broke free and fell, fortunately on the cushions. Still, it hit a bit hard and squealed.

Ariel went up with tame doves and parrots, setting them free under the ceiling and chasing them around, tumbling like a wind demon.

He flew up with boys and girls. The boys like it, while the girls squealed as loudly as the monkeys. He also flew around with platters of sweets and flowers, throwing the flowers to the spectators and deftly catching some of them before they fell.

When the raja ran out of ideas for indoor entertainment, they transferred to the park. The raja was particularly fond of one trick: Ariel had to slowly rise toward the dome of the tower at the very top of the palace, then fall from it toward the lake, head first, stop and roll over before the very surface of the water and return to the raja, "walking on water".

Ariel himself liked it. He rose along the wall, examining the ornaments, the reliefs, the cracks, the swallows' nests. Floor after floor flickered by, columns, galleries, balconies... He smiled at the people looking from the windows. One time he caught a rose held out by Shiama herself. He nodded to her and kept the flower.

He kept on going, higher and higher.

Finally he reached the top of the egg-shaped dome, under the sun, facing the gusts of wind. Above him was the blue sky, the vast country all around him. Swallows flew by swiftly. Lakes and ponds glittered below, like mirrors, groves and parks rippled with luxurious greenery. At these moments he wanted to sing. If only he could fly away! Where? To Lolita! But he could not. Not yet. The raja below looked as tiny as a bug. He was looking up, waiting for the jump. It was time.

It was strange – he rose from the ground calmly and happily, but just before the jump from this great height he felt fear and tightness in his chest, like a skydiver, afraid that his parachute may not open. What if his unusual ability to fly suddenly vanished?

Suppressing his instinct of self-preservation, Ariel dropped down and, after a bit, slowed down his fall a little. He was able to do it, which meant all was well! After that, he fell without fear.

"A man like that is worth more than his weight in gold!" the raja exclaimed in delight and went on to invent new amusements.

He thought of taking Ariel to the monkey zoo – that was what he called the ruins of an old palace, taken over by wild monkeys. They were so used to people that they accepted, or rather, quickly snatched food from their hands, but did not let anyone touch them. Ariel could catch the young monkeys. There would be so much confusion and fun!

He and Ariel could go hunting tigers. The raja imagined himself seated on his elephant, as the tiger leaped onto the elephant's neck, and Ariel dropped from above and plunged a dagger into the tiger's neck.

He could ask Ariel to catch birds in the woods... Fly through hoops decorated with flowers... Rise high above with a lantern at night and scatter blossoms... And why not try flying himself with Ariel's help?

The raja squinted with pleasure, imagining the endless line of new enticing amusements, to which he could invite important sahibs and wealthy neighbors. Everyone would see that the gods themselves served the glorious Raja Rajkumar!

Not only the raja, but all the other palace dwellers were enchanted by Ariel-Siddha. He was all anyone could talk about. "Did you hear what Siddha did yesterday? He walked on the ceiling upside down! Did you see him light fires in the air above the big lake last night?" Stories followed one after another. Everyone was astonished, many were jealous, yet others pitied him, "He is still in a cage, albeit a golden one." "If

I were him," one of the servants whispered to a friend, "I would have grabbed a sack of diamonds, as big as I could carry, and flown away!"

The rumors about Raja Rajkumar's flying man spread through the area. They reached Nizmat and his granddaughter and, eventually, the lawyer Dotaller.

CHAPTER TWENTY-THREE. MOHITA GATHERS DATA

There was only one man among the many living at the palace who watched Ariel glumly and with hidden anger. It was Mohita.

At first, he was glad of the extraordinary success of his find. But soon he noticed that the raja's attention was wholly absorbed by Ariel. Siddha-Ariel had pushed out everything and everyone else in his mind. Mohita has been forgotten by the ungrateful raja, as if Ariel indeed descended to the palace from heaven. Ariel was quickly becoming the new favorite. The raja showered him with valuable gifts, with which Ariel did not know what to do. Mohita was left alone and green with envy. Initially, he hoped that the changeful, capricious raja would soon tire of Ariel, as he did of all other novelties. But Ariel's gift inspired endless new ideas. One entertainment replaced another, one trick followed another, and they grew more and more fascinating. The raja sent out invitations to his neighbors – nabobs and other rajas – and to the important English officials, asking them to visit but not share what they had seen with reporters.

All this tortured the greedy and envious Mohita. He made a decision: one way or the other, he had to get rid of Siddha-Ariel.

At first he wanted to murder him secretly, but that was risky. He had to come up with a more sophisticated plan.

Soon, the circumstances offered him an opening.

Shiama was as interested in Ariel as everyone else. She was an impulsive woman, but kind, and she pitied him, understanding better than most how this rare "bird" felt in Rajkumar's gilded halls. Shiama paid a lot of attention to Ariel, took care of him, told her husband to let Ariel rest, and spoke to him in her room, whenever some urgent business distracted the raja from the games with his new favorite. She asked Ariel about his life, carefully followed the newspaper articles, in which anything new was said about the flying man, and made inquiries. She made a decision to investigate Ariel's past, find his family, and return him to his kin.

Ariel's room was on the same floor as hers, but, ordinarily, to get from one room to the other, one would have to go down to the ground floor, and then go up another staircase to the third floor. Ariel, of course, had a more convenient way. When Shiama came out to the balcony and called him, he simply flew over from his balcony to the rajina's. Shiama did not consider it necessary to hide these meetings. She believed that "Caesar's wife was above suspicion".

These visits were soon noticed by Mohita, whose duties included spying on everyone at the palace.

Mohita formed a plan. He secretly hated Shiama, and the feeling was mutual. They each had a good reason. Mohita disliked the rajina because she had great influence upon the raja, whereas Mohita wanted the master bent entirely to his own will and tried to achieve this by encouraging the tyrant's lowliest tendencies. Shiama loathed Mohita, because she recognized him for the mean, petty, and traitorous man that he was.

The hidden silent struggle between Shiama and Mohita went on for some time, sometimes bursting out into open altercations.

Finally, Mohita had a chance to kill two birds with one stone: get rid of the raja's new favorite and of Shiama. Then Mohita's influence with the raja would have no limits. The plan was all the easier, because the extremely self-centered and quick-tempered raja was also insanely jealous, as Mohita well knew. This nearly caused a huge scandal in Paris one time; an important sahib in India lost his head as the result, and the raja was forced to part with many of his "pretty stones" to cover up the matter.

To incite the raja's jealousy, to play on this age-old reliable emotion... But Mohita was cunning and careful. Jealousy alone might not have been sufficient, for the raja was very fond of Ariel and valued him highly. If he started checking and thinking, all would be lost. The clever Shiama would manage to talk her way out of it too. And who was Ariel? He was not a prince or an important sahib – he was not worthy of jealousy.

He had to act deftly and, first of all, damage Ariel's reputation in the raja's eyes, causing his displeasure and suspicion for some other reason. If he managed to change the master's mood against the new favorite, then Ariel would be "damned if he did and damned if he didn't." Mohita not only watched Ariel's every step, but ordered his assistants to do the same. His spying was perfectly organized.

Soon Mohita collected very satisfactory material. He noticed, and this was confirmed by his helpers, that Ariel gladly visited the pariahs among the servants. They reminded him about Nizmat, Lolita, and Sharad. Ariel liked children and visited them, making no exceptions even for the lowest castes: sweepers, skinners, cleaners of elephant stables. He entertained the children with flights and brought them fruit and sweets from the raja's table.

He was particularly attached to a sick boy, who looked like Sharad. He was the grandson of the old gardener. The boy dislocated his leg and could not walk. Ariel often picked him up, rose into the air, but not too high, and rocked him above the flower bed as if on a swing. The boy was delighted. He wrapped his thin little arms around Ariel's neck and laughed happily.

The raja's servants smiled while watching this scene and wiped tears. Their love and respect toward Ariel increased when the old gardener showed them an emerald and said, "Ariel gave me this to sell and use the money to invite a good doctor from the city. Our healer did nothing but torture my grandson, but he can't cure him."

"Where did Ariel get the emerald?" the servants wondered.

"It was the raja's gift," the gardener replied.

The emerald passed from hand to hand, sparkling against the dark skin.

"For a stone like that you can not only get a doctor but have a big wedding," they said.

"Whether he is a man or a god, nobody knows, but even gods don't care about us as much as Ariel does!"

When this strange creature flew out of his window and descended to them, the servants started telling Ariel about their needs and troubles with the sincerity of children. The raja's presents almost invariably went from Ariel to the servants.

"Excellent," Mohita thought. "Ariel throws the gifts of the raja himself left and right, and to whom? To these pariah dogs! The master cannot like this. I should mention something about missing a ring. A hint. Ariel can peek into any room on any floor, and fly in and out if no one is there. The servants complain to him. They see him as a protector. He consoles them, commiserates with them and, thus, corrupts them. We don't want this plague of public unrest from the cities to come here, do we? The raja won't stand for it!"

But Mohita hadn't told anything to the raja yet. He was still gathering data.

Soon, the following incident happened.

The raja was receiving some important foreign visitor, who was interested in the "exotics".

The raja showed the gladiator battle to the foreigner. The raja and the rajina often argued over these fights: the rajina could not stand this bloody entertainment and scolded both him and Mohita, but the battles continued in the rajina's absence.

This time, he invited the foreigner when the rajina went for a car ride.

Ariel sat next to the raja, having become his permanent companion. The raja held him back for "dessert", delaying his performance almost until the end of the visit.

The battle was at its height. Blood was flowing. The raja encouraged the fighters, his eyes flashing and his nostrils flaring.

One of them badly wounded the other. The wounded man fell. His opponent raised his weapon to deliver the final strike. But Ariel, right in front of the astonished guest, flew over his head and grabbed the fighter's hand. He ruined both the fight and his own performance with this unexpected flight.

The raja grabbed a spear from one of his bodyguards, intending to throw it at Ariel. Noticing this move, Ariel flew up above the arena.

"*Brut! Bete noire!* Savage beast!" the rajina's voice sounded.

Everyone looked up. In the confusion, no one noticed her automobile pull up to the fighting rink. The rajina was still in the car. Mohita arranged this in advance with her driver.

The raja bit his lip. When would the rajina finally stop interfering with his business? And how dare she call him names in front of the foreigner, and in French no less – the language known to the European guest?

"It's none of your business!" the raja exclaimed and threw the spear at the car, utterly enraged. The spear pierced the windshield, showering the driver with shards of glass.

The important guest wiped his sweaty face with a perfumed handkerchief, hiding a smile — he was fortunate to observe an interesting display of exotic morals!

Mohita rubbed his hands behind the raja's back. The first argument with Ariel! And not the last one with the rajina. Who knew? Perhaps it would be their last falling out as well. Mohita have long since stirred up the poison against the rajina. He hinted that she ruled the master, that the muster was kept under his wife's heel, that the other landlords were laughing behind his back. He suggested that the master would do very well by regaining his freedom and marrying the fifteen-year old daughter of the neighboring raja, the girl as lovely as the full moon and as gentle as a dove.

Even then, Mohita did not lay all his cards on the table, waiting for Ariel to make another misstep.

He finally got his chance.

From the very first day at the raja's house, Ariel never stopped missing Sharad, Lolita and Nizmat.

Even the joy of flight provided no comfort. At night, when the raja was asleep, Ariel came up to the window. The park sprawled serene in the moonlight. The palm fronds were motionless, as were the lilies and lotus flowers by the pond. The air was filled with dizzying fragrances. Perhaps, Lolita too was dreaming about him by the moonlight, and their gazes met upon the silvery disk in the middle of the sky. Ariel rose from the floor as lightly as a feather in the breeze and flew out the window. The inexpressible joy of flight overwhelmed him. He rose, first slowly, then faster and faster, along the palace wall. There was the roof... The familiar swallows' nests flickered by. Higher and higher! The entire countryside lay open before him, as if in a magical dream. He reached out his arms to the moon, to the blue expanses of the sky studded with stars, and to the blossoming land. The wall around the raja's estate gleamed white below. The palaces lost their grandeur from above and looked like a chaotic heap of fruit-like roofs of various shapes and sizes. Beyond them were the woods, with the road winding its way through the middle. Somewhere in these woods was Lolita's small cabin. If he rose higher, he could see the pond next to it. He was separated from the cabin by one small field.

"Lolita!" Ariel shouted out loud. He was so high up that no one could hear him.

Suddenly, forgetting everything – his promise to the raja and that he may have been watched – Ariel rushed down, toward the woods where he left his heart.

He found the cabin without any trouble. It was dark. Lolita and Nizmat slept inside, and Sharad was out on the porch. Ariel wanted to run to the boy he rescued and wake him up. But this wasn't the time. There would be an uproar at the raja's palace. And Piers was still looking for him and would pursue him again. Ariel sighed and gently kissed Sharad's head. He glanced around, flew up to the mango tree, gathered several pieces of fruit and set them down next to Sharad.

Then, saying good bye to his friends in his mind, he went back.

"He returned! Pity…" Mohita mumbled, sitting on the flat roof of a smaller palace where he lived with his family. "In any case, Ariel is breaking his promise by flying off somewhere in the middle of the night. I think I have enough information now!"

CHAPTER TWENTY-FOUR. DOWN COMES THE STORM

Catching the moment, when Ariel was visiting with Shiama, and the raja was particularly annoyed by something, Mohita approached him with all manner of grimaces, exaggerated sighs, and hints to state his case.

He was not accusing anyone and was not trying to prove anything. But it was his duty as a faithful servant to open his master's eyes at the things he, Mohita, did not approve of. Of course, there was nothing bad about them, but the facts could not be entirely ignored either.

As wily as ever, Mohita started listing the facts.

At first, he told the raja about Ariel – his gifts to the servants, the suspicious conversations, the night-time flights. He then carefully touched upon the rajina's behavior.

When she first saw Ariel, Shiama found him very handsome. Did she not say that? And right away – with such care! – she asked whether he was hungry. When Ariel flew around the palace and dropped flowers, the best roses fell into Shiama's lap. Was it a sign of respect from Ariel? Was it only respect? And what were the rajina's feelings when she caught the roses and pressed him to her face – or was it to her lips? Did she kiss them? With what delight, with what expression in her eyes she always watched the flying man! The raja did not see this because he himself was dazzled by Ariel. But Mohita's eyes saw everything. Did she not give Ariel a flower that one time, when this handsome youth flew up to the dome? And Ariel kept the rajina's rose.

Ariel spent too much time among the servants; perhaps he was conspiring against the raja, under the rajina's guidance. Who knew? Perhaps she was a part of it and threatened the master's life.

The rajina and Ariel arranged meetings in the open, as if for everyone to see how little she cared about her honor and about the good name of her noble husband. Ariel went to the *zenan*, forbidden by law to anyone else but the raja himself.

Blood rushed to the raja's head. His dark face became tinged with purple.

"It's a lie!" he croaked. "You are risking your head, Mohita!"

Mohita fell to his knees and exclaimed, "I would spare my head for the honor of the master of my soul. Go to the rajina and see for yourself. Go look at them coo together, like a pair of doves, as they prepare a dark plot against you!"

The raja rose, staggering from the overwhelming ire. His face was twisted. It was terrifying, as if hidden lightning lit it with bluish fire from within. Filled with rage and desire for revenge, he went to his wife's apartments. Mohita followed him.

The raja nudged the drape open.

Shiama and Ariel sat on the cushions by the balcony door. A platter of fruit sat on a lacquered little table between them. Ariel was telling something, while Shiama watched him and listened carefully.

A hoarse cry shook the air. Startled, Ariel and Shiama looked toward the drape and saw the raja.

The raja leaped at Ariel like a tiger and grabbed him by the throat. Shiama threw herself at the raja. Mohita whistled – everything had been prepared in advance. Servants rushed in.

"Tie up this son of a snake and this carrion!" the raja ordered the servants. "Put Ariel into the tower and this whore – into the cellar!"

The raja intended to say the other way around, but made a mistake in anger. Mohita realized that and wanted to correct him.

"Do I understand you properly, Master?"

The raja thought that Mohita was defending the rajina and shouted, "Don't argue!"

Mohita backed away and held his tongue.

Shiama straightened out. She was pale, her eyes flashed with rage.

"You garbage!" she exclaimed, looking at her husband with disdain. She then ran up to Mohita and slapped his face. "Scoundrel!"

The servants were reluctant to come closer and touch the rajina, some of them went to Ariel at Mohita's sign.

"Well? I'll skin you alive!" the raja screamed.

The servants started toward the rajina, nudging each other.

Shiama pulled a dagger from under her robe. The blade flashed.

"I shall kill myself before any of you touch me!" she shouted and pointed the tip of the dagger toward her chest.

The servants froze on the spot.

Ariel did not see what happened next. He was surrounded, tied up, picked up and carried off.

Ariel did not resist. He was astounded by the inner force with which Shiama stood up for herself, and felt numb.

He was thrown into the round tower and the door slammed shut behind him.

For some time, Ariel remained on the floor by the window, struck by what happened. His neck hurt and his head felt foggy.

When his thoughts cleared out somewhat, he started thinking. Mohita must have been watching him and told the raja about his flights beyond the raja's estate. But what was the rajina's guilt? What was she suspected of? So this was the end of his stay with the raja! This was the punishment for his indecision. He should have flown away from this cage a long time ago.

Poor kind rajina! Was she a victim of some vile suspicions and reports? She wasn't even allowed to defend herself. Could he fly away? The iron door was locked, and the window was heavily barred.

Ariel saw a portion of the park, the stone fence and beyond it, very close, the road.

A girl stood by the wall and watched the palace carefully.

Ariel was startled when he recognized Lolita.

The rumors that Ariel was living at the raja's palace had reached her and she sometimes made her way to the palace.

She had seen when Ariel flew up to the dome. She did not miss it when a beautiful woman handed him a flower, when he flew by her window, and her heart clenched. Could the dust on the road dream about the sun? Of course, Ariel must have found the happiness worthy of him at the palace!

But the mango that suddenly appeared near Sharad could have only been brought by Ariel. Which meant he came, he had not forgotten them! And Lolita wanted to see Ariel again, at least from a distance.

There was something wrong going on at the palace: there were excited shouts, people were running to and fro in the palace and in the park. But Ariel was not among them. Lolita was just about to leave, when she heard Ariel's voice, "Lolita! It's me, Ariel! If I get out of here, I shall come to you! Wait for me!" Just then, the bars on the door screeched, and he quickly sat down on the floor.

Lolita heard his words and shuddered. He was behind bars. What could it mean?

CHAPTER TWENTY-FIVE. THE MASTER CHANGES HIS MIND

The servants stuffed Ariel into a sack, tied the top and carried him somewhere. Mohita's assistant gave orders in a hoarse voice.

The sack was old and not very thick. Ariel saw the light and felt fresh breeze and realized he was being carried across the courtyard. Then the light faded, the air became stuffy and cooler. He was taken down some long corridors, and then down a steep staircase. There were more passages, and more steps. Finally, he was lowered onto cold stone tiles. The yellow light of a lantern flashed briefly. They opened the sack and silently put two heavy stones into it. Ariel noticed tears in the eyes of one of the servants, and silent compassion on the faces of others. But Mohita's assistant watched their every movement. Ariel saw the edge of the stone well. "So this is where the flying man will end his days," he thought bitterly.

Two servants tied the sack shut, lifted Ariel and threw him into the deep well with a groan.

In the palace, in Shiama's room, Mohita was crawling after his master, beating himself on the forehead with a fist and howling, "Have mercy, Master!"

The raja was rushing around the room, kicking Mohita away and screaming, "You, you! It's all your fault! Oh, you revolting, accursed snake! You have deprived me of the flying man – the best ornament of my palace and my favorite joy!

You have slandered him and the most honorable of all women! If Shiama dies, and she probably will..."

"Gods shall protect her, Master! The doctor said..."

"Oh, you cunning slave! How did your tongue turn to slander the best woman in the world? Why didn't your snake tongue become covered with sores? The lying dog that you are, you made me commit a crime. People do not lie before death, and she cried out to me..."

"She will not die, Master!"

"... that she was innocent and that it was you, disgusting villain, who lied about her. She opened my eyes." The raja clapped his hands.

"Have mercy, Master! Listen to me!"

"Just wait, you bastard! Take this despicable creature!" the raja addressed the servants. "Throw him into the cage with tigers! Oh, you shall provide me with worthy entertainment!"

The servants grabbed Mohita. He roared as if he was already in the cage.

But when they dragged him out into the other room, he stopped screaming and said quietly to the servants, "Don't throw me to the tigers today. Wait until tomorrow. Each of you shall receive a thousand rupees. Tomorrow, the raja's wrath shall pass, and he shall punish you if you rush to throw me into the cage. I can still be of use to him. And to you! Do you hear me, Bankim? Do you hear, Ganendra? A thousand rupees! Tomorrow, the raja will ask, 'Where is my dear Mohita?' But there will be no Mohita! 'Who dared to hurt him? Off with his head!' But if you don't kill me, he'll say, 'You did well to save my dear Mohita,' and reward you generously. Just in case, feed the tigers until they burst. I want pieces of meat sticking out of their mouths, so that these animals don't even want to look at me.

All this took place the evening prior to the day, when Boden, Piers, Dotaller, and Jane came to see the raja.

CHAPTER TWENTY-SIX. STRUGGLE FOR SURVIVAL

The well was deep. Having fallen for several seconds, Ariel tried to slow down. He succeeded, albeit with great difficulty. But could he go back up? The rocks were pulling him down.

The sack hit the water with a loud splash. Ariel shivered – the water was cold. To keep from wasting his strength, he concentrated on keeping just his head above water. The wet fabric barely let through any air, which was very stuffy and low on oxygen. Ariel was not only at risk of drowning, but also at risk of suffocation.

When the noise of his fall faded, voices sounded above him, "It's over! Pity!"

"You, Akshay, said that if he wasn't a god, he was related to god. If he was a god, he wouldn't have let us drown him like a newborn pup."

"It's him today, and maybe one of us tomorrow…"

That was the end of the eulogy. It was followed by the departing footfalls and the sound of a door being slammed shut.

Ariel pulled up with his mouth wide open. He felt as if his body was being torn in half. He even fainted for a moment, as the rocks continued pulling him down. He dropped back into cold water and came to.

"If I can't get out as soon as possible, I will certainly die," the thought flashed through his mind. Holding his breath, gritting his teeth and clenching his fists, he started rising once again, going more slowly this time, caught in a duel between two forces pulling up and down.

He kept telling himself not to faint, not to give in to the force pulling down, toward death.

Up, down, up again, and a little more, and a little more. Ariel was covered with sweat and shaking all over. He felt the salty taste of blood in his mouth. His eyes were burning.

Up! Up!

He was running out of strength. Should he end this terrible suffering and superhuman strain? His head filled with rustling, ringing and some kind of squealing. Perhaps, his blood vessels were bursting. Who was it? Where? The bluish steel of a dagger flashed and blinded him. He was falling, he could not survive.

But what if escape was near?

Ariel tried feeling for the walls of the well, but could not reach them. He kept rising and suddenly hit something with his head. Where was he? Did the servants cover the well with a stone slab? Then it was over!

With the last flicker of consciousness, Ariel realized – he was out of the well and hit the ceiling above it. He had to keep from falling back in.

He fainted.

Ariel must have been unconscious for a long time. When he woke up he was overjoyed to realize that he was lying on firm, dry ground.

Only a flying man could have made it out of that well alive! But he was still tied up and stuck in a sack with rocks.

He tried to untie his hands, but the knots were too tight. All he managed to do was to gnaw a small hole in the sack. Breathing became easier. What was next?

He crawled along the wall, turned around the corner, and made it to the door. He felt its outline through the sack, tried to push it, but the door did not open. He crawled further. Turned another corner. The wall kept going and going. It had to be a corridor. Perhaps, it would lead him to freedom. Sometimes resting, sometimes half-fainting, Ariel moved slowly forward. The sack started falling apart. The ropes were slowly loosening from the movement.

Suddenly, he felt a stream of fresh air flowing from somewhere into this warm, stuffy dungeon, and soon found an opening. He tried crawling through it, but only his head fit through.

He crawled further.

He passed several such openings that apparently served for ventilation. Finally, he found one that was wide enough for him to get in. He squeezed through until he reached the other side. The old sack finally split in half and the stones fell out. Ariel rose up lightly, flew up to another turn and once again felt a stream of fresh air.

Finally outside, he happily took a deep breath.

Which way? Ariel turned toward sunrise. East was that way, west – behind him, south to the right, north to the left. Which way? To Lolita, of course, to Nizmat and Sharad! He turned toward the road.

As he flew over the park and the well, from which he rescued the little boy, Ariel heard someone's astonished cry.

"He really is a brother to the gods!" the servant exclaimed, shaking his head. It was Akshay. "Go, fly away, my boy!" he greeted Ariel. "I won't tell anyone that I saw you! But you must make sure you won't get caught anymore! Your heavenly relatives are not too keen on helping you out during hard times!"

Ariel didn't hear these words and did not see the man by the well – he was in too much of a hurry. While he was flying without any additional weight, he felt that his strength was waning once again. All the tribulations of the previous day, the terrible night, the superhuman exhaustion… No, he could not make it to good Nizmat's cabin.

Ariel landed in the shrubs by the road and fell into uneasy sleep.

CHAPTER TWENTY-SEVEN. AN UNEXPECTED FIND

At sunrise, the road became crowded with peasants, traveling monks, and merchants with heavily laden donkeys.

It was almost noon, when a dusty automobile appeared on the road, with three man and a young woman seated in it. At the sight of the car, the frightened peasants left the road and bowed.

"Stop, James," one of the sahibs said, addressing the driver, when the car approached a man lying by the roadside. "This looks like a crime. See that bloodied head?"

The girl in the car grew pale.

"Why do we care, Mister Dotaller?" an old sahib with an owl-like face objected. "Bodies are found on the roads of India every day. They are savages! Keep going, James!"

The car pulled forward.

"Wait, James!" Dotaller shouted. "Go back. We can't just leave him, Mister Boden. Look – this is a white man. Perhaps he is an Englishman and is still alive. After all, these locals are only too happy to dispose of a sahib. I don't care what you think, but I am going to check."

The car stopped.

"He is groaning! He is alive!" Dotaller exclaimed. "There are ropes around his wrists, I need to untie him," he continued, leaning forward and cutting off the bits of rope, handling them with disgust. "Hey, you! Somebody! Come here!" he shouted to the peasants standing nearby.

His beckoning gesture was clear even to those who did not speak English, but no one moved.

"Idiots! Cowardly morons!" Dotaller cursed. "James, be so kind, please help me!"

At the same moment, Piers cried out in terror, "It's him!"

"Who?" the girl asked quickly, growing even paler.

"Him... your unfortunate brother Ariel... Aurelius Galton..."

Jane gasped and fell back against her car seat.

Boden and Piers ran to Ariel.

The men carried Ariel to the car.

Jane clasped her hands and silently looked at her brother. Ariel was unconscious.

"Let's go, James!" Dotaller commanded.

The car horn beeped. The crowd staggered away and the car moved.

When the crowd of peasants remained behind them and the automobile sped up, a passing girl in a worn sari held out her arms and shouted, "Ariel!"

Ariel's face filled with joy, he smiled weakly, but his eyes remained closed.

"That is just great! Some vagrant from the street knows his name!" Jane thought.

"I will have to look into this!" Piers thought, looking back at the poor girl in surprise.

CHAPTER TWENTY-EIGHT. HE FLEW AWAY

Ariel was brought into a hotel at the small town not far from the raja's residence. He was put to bed, and a doctor was sent for.

Ariel was delirious. Jane remained at her brother's side. She gave him water, rubbed his temples with fragrant vinegar and, watching his exhausted face, thought, "I hope he lives!"

Dotaller thought, "I hope he dies!"

Piers thought, "I won't let him out of sight ever again!"

Boden… Without the owl-like eyes of his partner, Boden had completely lost his ability to think logically. "There has to be a way to benefit from this. But how?"

Having examined Ariel, the doctor said in English, "It's a fever. Possibly due to emotional strain. He has been through some great shock."

"Quite," Piers chimed in from the corner.

"Is it dangerous?" Jane asked.

"No, Miss. If it's solely due to his nerves, then it is not dangerous, but…"

The doctor was concerned about the bleeding from nose, ears and mouth the patient seemed to have sustained recently. He could not explain it and tried not to reveal his confusion.

Having prescribed a medicine, he rushed to leave. Piers remained at Ariel's' side and listened to his delirium.

"The dagger… Shiama… She killed herself… What lies! Lolita… But I can fly… We'll fly away together…"

"Is he talking about that miserable little beggar on the road?" Jane thought.

Piers said to her, "You can now see for yourself, Miss, that your brother is mentally ill. His mania is his belief that he can fly like a bird."

At the sound of Piers' voice, Ariel shuddered and his face twisted, he opened his eyes and screamed in terror, "Piers! Bharava? Dandarhat again?" and fainted again.

"What is he talking about? What is bothering him?" Jane asked, frightened by her brother's scream and his face. "What is Dandarhat?"

"People often talk nonsense when they are delirious, whatever occurs to them at the moment," Piers replied, nevertheless stepping away from the bed. He stood where Ariel could not see him.

The doctor was right – Ariel was merely suffering from shock. As it often happened in such cases, fire was defeated by fire – seeing Piers and hearing his voice, the thought of possibly being back at Dandarhat reawakened Ariel's instinct of self-preservation and broke through his delirious state. Ariel soon regained consciousness. Having learned to conceal his thoughts and feelings at Dandarhat, he decided not to show that he was awake, and started faking delirium, all the while watching his surroundings.

He noticed a pretty girl. "Probably a nurse," he thought. Having surreptitiously surveyed the room, he was relieved to discover that he was not at Dandarhat. So, he still had a chance to run away from Piers, who clearly managed to track him down!

Someone's excited voices could be heard from the adjacent room. Dotaller and Boden were arguing over Ariel. Piers couldn't stand it and went to join them. Only the girl remained.

If only she would leave too! The window was open, Piers didn't bother shutting it, believing Ariel to be gravely ill. Should he try and fly away? Did he have enough strength? He was still very weak, even though a bowl of hearty broth was very helpful. In any case, what had he to lose? He was at Piers' mercy, it couldn't get any worse.

Ariel rose over the bed, lying horizontally, as he was, still covered with a sheet. The girl screamed. Ariel circled the room and flew out through the window.

Hearing Jane's scream, the others ran in.

"He flew away. Or am I sick and delirious too? Aurelius rose from the bed and flew out."

Piers ran to the window and saw Ariel against the blue sky, high up above the palm trees.

"This rascal tricked me again!" he yelled in rage.

"Then it's true. My God! But this is impossible. Aurelius flies? My brother, Aurelius Galton is a flying man?"

"Yes, yes, yes!" Piers shouted into the girl's face. "He flies and he flies away, damn him! I made him into a flying man, much to my own detriment, and yours as well, if you must know."

CHAPTER TWENTY-NINE. THE AIR BATTLE

Ariel flew so fast he was out of breath. He grabbed the edges of the sheet and wrapped it around himself to keep it from billowing around him and slowing him down. One corner broke free and flapped like a white wing. Residents of a provincial town below watched the strange white bird in astonishment.

He could see the flat roofs, the narrow winding streets, the gardens, and beyond the city – a tree-covered mountain, a sandy valley, and more greenery in the distance.

Having broken free of yet another prison, Ariel no longer considered where to go, no longer picked and chose the direction. He just wanted to get away as far as possible.

Strong hot wind flew in from the left and started carrying Ariel off to the side, interfering with his flight. Ariel suddenly saw the smoky-gray clouds billowing from beyond the blue foggy horizon. A storm was coming. Ariel changed direction and flew even faster.

Having traveled for about an hour, he felt tired. The sun was scorching. He was hungry and thirsty.

He had to land and rest.

He looked down to choose a spot. Railway glinted below, factory smokestacks rose between the tall red-brick buildings, surrounded by the shacks of the workers' village. No, he had to get further away from people!

The endless fields beyond were spotted with copses of trees. The silver band of a river flowed across them. That way!

The fields remained behind him. He could already see the profusion of reeds ahead. Could anyone see him here? He should land and pick out a secluded place to rest.

Suddenly, there was a noise and flapping of winds above his head. Ariel saw an enormous eagle that descended so low that his wings created a breeze and a deafening noise. The bird's bright eyes were leveled at Ariel, the predatory hooked beak was half-open, the talons were spread. Ariel dashed to the side, the eagle followed.

The eagle dropped toward him swiftly, and the man evaded the strikes just as swiftly. He circled and tried to grab the bird by the wings or by the neck from above. But the eagle was just as fast.

At one point, the eagle managed to scratch Ariel's leg. Ariel became enraged and kicked the bird in the back, making it tumble in the air.

He was trying to learn his opponent's tactics.

He soon realized that the eagle was at his fastest when he dropped down with his wings folded, and could also fly forward with great speed. However, it took him some time to gain speed when the bird turned, its large wings becoming more of a hindrance. Going from horizontal flight to vertical ascent took the longest. The difference was measured in mere seconds, perhaps even fractions of seconds, but it was enough to be decisive. The safest thing was to gain altitude.

The enormous bird and its human opponent started rising higher and higher, tumbling through the air. Both were becoming tired.

Ariel, who was already fatigued, was having a tough time. Several times, he was inches away from the eagle's claws, as the bird struck him in the face with its tough feathers. Finally, Ariel received such a hit on the head with the eagle's wing, that he momentarily fainted, but then recovered, flew higher and grabbed the eagle's neck. The eagle too pulled up, trying to break free but unsuccessfully. The frightened bird, its enemy in tow, flew directly toward the mountains beyond the woods.

Ariel tried controlling its flight by covering the eagle's eyes and turning its head. But the bird did not understand what was required and started dashing about haphazardly. Ariel abandoned the idea.

There was a river down below, where Ariel could get water – that was the main thing.

They landed in a clearing not far from the river. Ariel instantly flew up and vanished in the reeds. The eagle, having crashed heavily into the thick grass, remained there for some time with its wings spread, its beak opening and closing, staring before itself with dazed eyes. Then the defeated king of the air shook himself off, folded his wings and took off.

CHAPTER THIRTY. ALONE IN HEAVEN AND ON EARTH

When the flapping of wings faded away, Ariel heard the sound of a flute, looked down and saw a peaceful scene.

A herd of buffalo grazed on the silty river bank. A large, bluish-black bull with rounded horns walked into the mix of water and silt up to his neck, and the others followed, and soon all one could see above water was their flat noses.

Half-naked farm boys were playing on the hill – making houses out of clay, building walls, palaces, and buffalo, arming their clay soldiers with spears made out of reeds. Others wove baskets from grass and caught grasshoppers, yet others made necklaces of black and red nuts, caught frogs, played hand-made flutes and sang songs with strange trills and changes. Ariel forgot about his thirst and hunger and watch the shepherds curiously for some time. He felt jealous. They were happy in their own way. They passed their childhood years in the middle of nature, no one was chasing them, torturing them, or frightening them, as they did with children at Dandarhat. Ariel had nothing to remember about his childhood, save for the distant, nearly faded memories about the house in the foggy city, the room, the carpet, the toys, and the little blond girl. Even these memories were darkened by the sinister figure of the man who crushed his toys and his childhood.

Ariel suddenly remembered his illness and his recent delirium. It only happened the day before! Among the faces surrounding his bed he saw an old man, who resembled that man in black, even though he was dressed in a white suit traditionally worn by Europeans in India. Could it be real? The sinister old man with the pointy, beak-like nose and owl-like eyes was standing next to Piers. Why was he in the room? There was another man, tall and clean-shaven, who also stared at Ariel with hatred. What did these people want and what did they have in common? Only the girl looked at him with compassion. She was probably as kind as his friends. Still, there were so few kind people in the world.

The distant roll of thunder returned Ariel to reality.

The air was scorching hot and very stuffy. He once again remembered that he was hungry and thirsty. As if on purpose, the little shepherds abandoned their games, settled down in a circle and started eating, passing around rice cakes, coconuts and grapes.

Should he ask them? But if they saw him fly in with the eagle, they would run away in terror. They might, but even if they ran away, they would leave the food behind. Ariel rose, pulled his sheet around himself and approached the children.

The boys treated a strange white man cautiously.

"Hello, brothers! I am a poor acrobat. Would you like to see a trick?" Ariel asked.

He stood on his hands, then rose up on his fingers, then rested on just the index finger of his left hand. Having done that for a minute, he flipped back onto his feet.

The children were delighted.

They had never seen a single gymnast at the fare do such a fantastic trick. When Ariel jumped and did several flips in the air, their joy overflowed all boundaries. They fought to offer him bread, raisins and coconuts.

Ariel had some water and a good meal.

Thunder rumbled closer and closer. Ariel wanted very much to stay with the children, but the fear of Piers urged him on.

Having said good bye to the children, Ariel went deep into the forest. Once the trees completely obscured the river bank, the children, and the buffalo, he rose above the woods and looked around carefully.

The clouds have already covered half the sky and cast a deep shadow over the fields he had just passed. The wind blew in strong gusts. It was just as well. The same wind that was pushing forth the clouds would help him fly further away from his pursuers. Ariel rose higher. The dark blue clouds were right above his head.

Suddenly, hurricane-strength wind swept Ariel up, threw him down, spun him, then carried him up, right into the heart of the clouds. Ariel tried struggling with the wind but immediately realized that it was impossible. To keep from wasting his strength, he decided to surrender to the cyclone. After all, there was no great risk to him. He couldn't fall down and crash. Once the storm subsided and could no longer carry him, he could go back to flying on his own.

Having made his body weightless, Ariel felt no wind whatsoever. He could breathe easily. There wasn't the slightest air movement around him. "That's because I am flying at the same speed as the cyclone," Ariel realized.

He looked down and was startled – despite flying at a great height, he could still see fields, mountains, forests, rivers, and villages rushing underneath him with incredible speed. When he looked up he thought he saw the blue mountains, brown rocks, and black crevasses interwoven with blinding lightning – it all seemed to be falling on top of him. Suddenly, everything crashed, surrounded him and spun him out of control. Where was sky? Where was earth? Everything was covered with gray murk, with flashes of lightning, thunder, and sudden sheets of rain falling from the top, from the bottom, and sometimes sideways. The winds twirled and tumbled him like a leaf. Water poured into his ears, mouth, and nose, and his head felt foggy.

He finally found a downward draft. Rain and wind seemed to stop suddenly – he was falling with them. But the moment he tried slowing down, waves of air and water crashed upon him and pushed him further down.

Suddenly, he saw the ground very close. No, it wasn't the ground but a limitless dark sea, lit by lightning. Did the cyclone carry him into the ocean? How long could he survive in the water? No, it wasn't the ocean. With another flash, Ariel saw treetops and roofs. He was flying above a flooded valley.

Suddenly, the golden ray of the setting sun fell upon a small island. There! He had to make it there no matter what!

Overcoming the wind, Ariel flew toward the scrap of land. He saw the cabins of a poor village. The clouds once again hid the sun, but the hurricane was over, having flown further on. The wind had subsided. It was still raining, although not quite as much.

Ariel nearly fell by a vine-covered gazebo and heard someone's heavy breathing nearby.

A buffalo with glossy bluish-black skin lay nearby, having probably swam here from afar and exhausted by his struggle with the elements.

Having rested a little, Ariel splashed across the frog-filled puddles and mud toward a path, hopefully leading to human habitation. Bamboo creaked under the last few gusts of wind.

He reached a cabin. The grass roof had fallen in. Ariel walked onto the porch and entered the house, spooking a gray lizard at the doorway. Small scorpions scampered across the floor, making a ticking sound. The walls were covered with mold. A narrow ladder led to the roof.

A naked old man sat in the corner. He could be mistaken for a statue, so still he was, seated in the pose of deep contemplation. He was nothing but a skin-covered skeleton with a long white beard.

"*Saniasi!*" Ariel called out to him.

The old man did not emerge from his meditation right away. Finally, he raised his head, looked at Ariel with his unseeing pale blue eyes and said, "The joy of discovering the infinite lies in the finite!" He looked down once again.

Ariel knew that he would not find help there. He left.

It was now completely dark. Having walked across the village, Ariel discovered that it was half-ruined and deserted.

Only one cabin was lit by a flickering lantern, with four white ghosts moving within – these were women who usually came to attend a dead body before the funeral.

Ariel suddenly felt such loneliness and loss, that he cried for the first time since the black man stepped on his toys.

Despite the nightfall, he pulled up and flew over the dead, water-covered valley, trying not to look down.

The last few clouds fell beyond the horizon.

A bright star flashed in front of Ariel in the endless night sky. He flew toward it as if to a lighthouse.

To the stars! As far as possible from earth and its people!

CHAPTER THIRTY-ONE. IN THE JUNGLE

Ariel woke up under the ceiling of a half-ruined temple and didn't realize right away where he was. Then he remembered the dead flooded desert with stars reflected in it. He flew over it for a long time, almost all night. Finally, a black strip of a forest appeared on the horizon beyond the dark-blue expanse of water. The promise of solid ground and rest pushed Ariel to fly faster.

When he reached the edge of the woods, he was so tired that he didn't bother looking for a dry spot, but flew up to a large sprawling tree and settled in its branches as if in a nest. He leaned against the trunk and fell asleep instantly.

He was woken up by the first rays of sunlight and was surprised to discover that he was hanging in the air next to the tree. He must have pushed away from his support in his sleep. Fortunately, he made his body weightless just before he fell asleep, which was why he didn't fall to the ground but continued hanging in the air. That was a useful discovery – he could sleep in the air! This ability would come very useful later.

The air was filled with heavy fog, pierced by the crimson-orange sunbeams. Birds were already up and singing all around him, monkeys played and squealed. Down below, a giant cobra curled up in the sun among the thick gnarled tree roots. He shuddered to think what would have happened, had he fallen down in his sleep!

The cobra drank some water from a puddle, lifted its head in a rocking movement, looked around and saw a colorful bird in the grass.

Ariel saw that the bird was in danger and wanted to shoo it away, but the cobra was upon its prey in one lightning-quick motion and swallowed it whole.

"Piers hunts me the same way," Ariel thought. "But the cobra hunts because it's hungry. What does Piers want with me?"

Ariel too was hungry, and it was time to think about food.

He once again rose above the tree tops and saw that he was at the very edge of the wild, primitive jungle. As far as the eye could see, there were enormous trees, their foliage rippling like waves in a sea of green. Ariel flew over the greenery. In the middle of a clearing, he saw ruins of a temple with crude columns, wrapped in vines. Thick brush grew all around it.

It wouldn't be a bad place to live. Ariel landed through an opening in the half-collapsed roof.

The air was moist and still. There was enough of the roof left to protect him from cold and tropical rains. In the corner of the less-damaged portion of the temple was a black statue of seated Indra three times taller than a man. The god's hands rested on his knees. One leg was lowered to the ground, the other was curled underneath him. His eyes were half-closed. There was a cone-shaped miter on his head and a necklace around his neck. To his sides were statues of minor gods. Ariel thought he could make his bed in Indra's lap by piling on branches, leaves, and moss.

The statue was in a long narrow room. To the left were columns, separating this space from the adjacent one, but the right side was wide open, its ceiling supported only by four square columns. There was nothing there to keep out wild animals.

But then, was he not surrounded by animals anyway?

Ariel flew out of the temple and went from one tree to the next, like a bee looking for honey. Much to his joy, he discovered that there were plenty of trees bearing edible fruit in this forest. A spring of fresh water bubbled nearby. There was a reason why the temple was built in this spot! The grass by the creek was trampled by animals that came there to drink.

By evening, Ariel was ready to move in. He even managed to gather and set aside some fruit in case of bad weather, and made a bed in Indra's lap out of branches and moss. Shortly after sunset, Ariel realized he wasn't the only tenant of the temple. In addition to scorpions, lizards, and bats he noticed during the day, the ruins teemed with snakes. They crawled in after hunting and curled together in bundles to keep warm. Soon, the entire floor was covered with tangles of snakes, hissing and settling down for the night. Rust-colored fruit bats flew about in swarms, their wings brushing against the new neighbors. Sometimes they dove all the way to the floor, disturbing the snakes and causing them to hiss. Sleeping in Indra's lap in such close proximity with countless snakes was beginning to look dangerous. Remembering his morning discovery, Ariel decided to sleep under the ceiling over Indra's head.

Sometimes, the voices of nocturnal animals and birds woke him up, but he soon became used to them.

Ariel gradually settled into his new life in the jungle. During the first few days he was glad that he flew so far away from his pursuers, finding the company of wild animals and snakes superior. But in the evenings, before he fell asleep, he keenly felt his loneliness and his isolation and remembered his few friends – Lolita, Nizmat, and Sharad. But it was too early to think about going back to them. He had to wait until Piers became convinced that Ariel was gone without a trace and seized his search.

No longer afraid of being seen, he could now fully enjoy flying.

Until then, all he ever did was fly away from someone or amuse others.

In the jungle, he could fly for the sake of flying.

At dawn, Ariel swiftly rose into the blue expanse. The heavy, damp air of the jungle was replaced by the light, fresh air of the sky. Ariel sang his morning song along with the early birds.

Sometimes he made long trips. He admired the changing light in the clouds and the charm of moonlit nights with their sense of freedom, ease and vast space.

He flew around for hours, until his body reminded him that he was a prisoner of earth after all. He felt tired, thirsty, hungry, or sleepy, and had to return to his new dwelling.

One starry night, Ariel tried to sleep high up above the woods. When he woke up, he saw that the wind carried him far off to the side, and he barely found his way back. Ever since then, he made no more attempts to sleep in the air.

Days passed, and Ariel became more and more used to the jungle. He studied the habits of birds and animals, made friends with some and became enemies with others. One time, a tiger tried to ambush him by the creek and jumped at him. Ariel barely managed to fly off to the side. The tiger leaped again, enraged by the man hanging in the air, and Ariel flew higher. The tiger started jumping up madly, trying to get to his prey. Ariel couldn't help but tease the beast, until the animal became utterly frustrated by his defeat and ran off into the jungle. The flying man followed him for some time, hollering wildly for added effect. Monkeys and parrots happily took part in mocking the king of the jungle.

Several monkeys, after running away from Ariel and pelting him with whatever they could find, finally became his friends and came to visit him, knowing he set aside some of the best fruit for them. Two parrots often accompanied him during his flights across the woods, greeting him with the rolling, "Arr-r-riel! Ar-r-riel!"

He taught them to say the names of his friends and he felt as if they weren't far away.

He had seen the terrible battles of elephants and buffalo with tigers and watched migrations of enormous herds of wild animals. From above, they looked as small as rats, and their trunks – like thick tails curled up over their heads. At a closer distance, he could hear the dull thudding of their mighty feet, the crackling of broken trees, the strikes of the tusks, the dry rustling of their wrinkled skin and trunks running into each other, the growling and the roaring. He saw hundreds of flapping ears, raised trunks, and moving tails. He saw the enormous old elephants with white tusks, leaves and branches stuck in the folds of their skin. Some had only one tusk and ragged scars around their necks – the remnants of past battles. He also saw the scampering black calves, only two-three feet tall, running under the bellies of their mothers and teasing young males with barely showing tusks.

Without realizing it, Ariel was turning into a wild man. His hair grew longer and he went everywhere naked, having carefully preserved his shirt and sheet under the rocks.

For days on end, he flew from one tree to the next searching for food, surrounded by birds and monkeys, and always rising higher at the slightest sign of danger. He may have turned into a complete savage and ended his days in the jungle. But it did not happen thanks to the parrots he tamed.

"Lolita! Nizmat! Sharad!" they shouted from morning until night, and these words resonated in his heart both with joy and with reproach, forcing him to think about his future.

The incident at the raja's palace and seeing Piers again left deep scars in Ariel's heart. He seemed to quickly pass from his artificially cultivated infantilism to maturity, although he himself could not quite explain the change in himself.

Until recently, he was nothing but a passive tool in the hands of others. All he learned at Dandarhat was to lie and conceal his thoughts and moods. Having escaped from Dandarhat, he lived in fear of once again ending up at Piers' hands. Paralyzed by this fear, he didn't give any thought to any sort of active struggle, any way to win the right to live his life the way he wanted and not the way desired by others.

Fear brought him into this wilderness, deprived him of the company of people, some of whom were good and kind, and sentenced him to loneliness. Eventually, human pride and outrage awoke in him. No, he would not stay in the jungle! He would return to people and fight for his right to live among them!

Why shouldn't he take advantage of his unusual gift? A flying man could do a lot! He did not know yet, what exactly, for he knew so little about the outside world. "Time will tell what needs to be done," Ariel decided and started preparing for the road.

He found a nut, whose sap colored his skin brown. He looked both like an Indian and like a very tanned European. The color paled somewhat after bathing, but didn't fade for a long time. He examined his shirt and sheet, washed them, and even tried ironing them with rocks, warmed up in the sun. One morning, having gathered a small quantity of fruit, he set out on his journey.

CHAPTER THIRTY-TWO. THE NEW CONVERT

Pastor Edwin Kingsley took off his glasses, sighed, leaned back in his chair and looked up. On the wall before him hung a portrait of the king with his long Anglo-Saxon face and large, slightly bulging eyes that ran in the family. Next to it hung the portraits of the viceroy in India, the severe-looking lord with thin lips, and the Bishop of Canterbury in full ceremonial garb. The king and the viceroy's heads were turned to the side, as if turning away from the pastor, and the bishop was looking him straight in the eye with reproach, or so it seemed to Kingsley, the missionary who failed.

What would His Eminence, who until then held Kingsley in favor, say when he saw his latest report?

Pastor Kingsley had pored over that report for three weeks, trying to present the situation in as good a light as possible.

Initially, the conversion of Indians to Christianity went very well. In his reports, Kingsley implied that the reasons for such great success were his hard work as a missionary and his talent as a preacher.

The true reason was altogether different. The sheep, the pagans the pastor attracted into the flock of Christ, came from the lowest, most despised castes. Conversion to Christianity was beneficial to them, for it somewhat improved their dismal situation. The important role was played by the silver crucifixes and cheap gifts the new converts received on their baptismal day. But suddenly, everything changed. Some Indian religious society, concerned by the number of converts to Christianity, came up with a special purification ritual for the pariahs, which elevated them a step higher in society. While the novelty caused some objections from the more conservative Hindus, it was very successful. Many pariahs now preferred purification to baptism. Kingsley's missionary success came to an end. It was becoming harder and harder to attract new proselytes. Those who had already converted were beginning to renege.

Pastor Kingsley found himself in a very difficult position. He had lost his appetite and felt restless. During the day, he labored over the exhausting report and at night he tried to invent the means by which to improve matters. He wrote eloquent sermons and took missionary trips to the most distant villages of his parish, but nothing helped. These pagans and idol-worshippers could only be impressed by a miracle that would prove the superiority of the Christian God. But where was he to get such a miracle?

"John! Breakfast for Mister Kingsley!" the pastor heard his sister, a spinster, Miss Florence Kingsley.

A Hindu boy entered, carrying a tray with a steaming coffee pot, a cup, and a plate of fried eggs and toast.

The boy was the godson of "Aunt Florence" (as everyone called the pastor's sister), Paresh, whose Christian name was John. He wore a silver belt – the gift from his godmother and the main reason for becoming baptized, a silver crucifix around his neck, and an amulet left to him by his late parents. Paresh-John absolutely refused to part with it.

As he poured his coffee, the pastor looked at the crucifix and the amulet and sighed, "They are all the same way. A crucifix and an amulet worn over their hearts, and in their hearts... who knows?"

"I believe the pastor is busy just now," he heard the voice of his daughter Susannah from the next room. She was speaking to someone in Hindustani.

Mister Kingsley perked up. What if this was some local, who had heard his sermon and decided to convert? Forgetting his breakfast, the pastor quickly threw a robe over his pajamas and hurried into the hallway.

A slender, dark-skinned youth with a handsome face and long hair stood before him. He had an overall air of a hermit.

He was wearing nothing but a long shirt and a strange white cape. These locals wore all manner of odd things!

"Are you here to see me?" the pastor asked.

"Yes," the young man replied modestly, looking down. "I wanted to speak to you, Mister. But, perhaps, this is not a good time?"

Susannah, a girl of twenty, with her head shaved after a bout with typhoid, looked glumly between her father and the young man.

The pastor, realizing that the youth came to have a serious talk, invited him into the study.

The unexpected guest introduced himself as Binoy. He was a Hindi, an orphan. He wanted to dedicate his life to serving God. He knew something about Christianity, but wanted to study it further. What was it that he did not like about his native religions? Their gods showed none of themselves in a tangible way, and never came to help people.

The pastor frowned and thought, "He is fairly smart for a local, with a practical mind. These cunning folk demand portents and miracles. Such people are hard to deal with. Still, it might be possible to prove to him that God's existence is evident not only through miracles. Must they all be obsessed with miracles?! The main thing is to get him to stay and baptize him no matter what, even if it requires something better than a silver crucifix. I must have new converts for my report!"

"We shall talk about this some more, my friend," the pastor said gently. "But in order to do that, we must be able to meet often. Where do you live?"

"I am a wanderer, seeking a true God," the guest replied.

The pastor thought about it and declared solemnly, "You shall stay with me, Binoy! Yes, yes. I can always find a warm corner and a bowl of rice for a man seeking God! Florence!" he shouted. When the bony, gray-haired woman in a black dress entered, he said, "This is Binoy. I hope he becomes one of your godchildren. He shall live with us. Please take him to the attic."

Aunt Florence looked the young man over curiously and nodded, "Come long!"

When they left, Susannah ran into the pastor's study.

"Listen, father,"s he said in agitation. "I think you are going a bit too far in your missionary zeal. Could you not have let that vagrant stay with the groundskeeper? These dirty Gypsies are all carriers of infection. It's bad enough that I had typhoid, I don't want to pick up cholera and plague as well!"

"Not a single hair shall fall from a man's head without God's will," Mister Kingsley said piously, trying to conceal his embarrassment.

"Not a single hair! My head is already shaved. You can save this for your sermons. I don't want our house to be invaded by beggars!"

"But it is necessary, my child. What am I to do? Each profession has its dangers. What if I were a doctor? After all, I do go to administer the last rites to the dying."

He usually gave in to his daughter, but this time he turned unexpectedly stubborn. Binoy stayed.

Ariel spent some time coming up with a plan. While still at Dandarhat, he already had a vague notion as to what he was being prepared for, when he was converted into a flying man. Clearly, they wanted to demonstrate him as a miracle to strengthen the faith of others. But why not use that role for his own purposes? He had to find a temporary shelter, look around and learn more about people, perhaps save a little money to begin an independent life.

His further plans were unclear as of yet. They changed frequently, but Lolita, Nizmat, and Sharad always figured prominently in them.

When he was flying over a small town, Ariel saw the tall bell tower and came up with the first step for rejoining the society of people.

He quickly sensed Susannah's animosity. She avoided him and barely returned his greetings. Aunt Florence, however, whom Susannah nicknamed "missionary in a skirt", became Binoy's chief benefactress.

In the evenings, the pastor held long talks with the young man. Yielding to his daughter, he no longer invited Binoy to the study, but went to see him in the attic, where Binoy lived the life of a hermit. He was very modest in his needs and food, and spent entire days over the Bible and the Gospel.

Binoy's ardor and quick learning impressed and delighted the pastor, who had no idea that his student had already learned the history of religion – the only thing that was taught thoroughly at Dandarhat.

Soon, Binoy was baptized and received another name – Benjamin, or Ben, as the pastor and Aunt Florence called him. He remained with the pastor to continue strengthening his faith, and did so well at it that he nearly caused his mentor a stroke.

CHAPTER THIRTY-THREE. "MIRACLE"

It happened on a Sunday.

The pastor was delivering a sermon in the half-empty church, talking about faith, about miracles, and about divine intervention in the affairs of men.

"God is omnipotent, and if He does not come to people's aid, it is only because they do not ask Him for it with sufficient amount of faith. For I tell you truthfully, the Holy Writ says that if you have but a mustard seed's worth of faith and say to a mountain, 'Come here,' it shall do so; and nothing shall be impossible for you."

At those words, Ben-Ariel, who was sitting in the front pew, suddenly walked into the middle of the church, clutched his psalter firmly, looked up and exclaimed, "I believe, Lord, that you shall act upon my faith! Raise me above ground!"

Everyone watched, as the youth's body shook and rose up into the air, his feet ending up about two feet off the floor. He went up and down several times, thanking God each time he lowered to the floor.

The pastor had to grab the lectern to keep from falling down. He went pale and his lower jaw was shaking.

The church became so quiet that one could hear swallows flying by the windows. People seemed to turn into stone. What followed next was sheer mayhem. The walls shook from people's hysterical, fanatical screams. Everyone present jumped up from their seats. Some panicked and ran for the doors, trampling each other, others fell to their knees before

Ben, reaching out to him, yet others beat themselves on the chest, laughed, cried, and exclaimed, "There is God! There is God! He exists!"

If only Piers could see this! There was a good reason the London headquarters placed such high hopes into the flying man.

Ariel stood there, smiling awkwardly, as if he had not yet realized what happened.

The pastor raised a hand, trying to restore order, but he himself was as shocked as the others. He gestured with a shaking hand, then slid down from the lectern, as his legs no longer held him, then gasped and sat down on the floor, reeling from the miracle.

***

Susannah, dressed in her riding habit and black bonnet, was riding home on her dun-colored little horse after her morning ride. She enjoyed galloping across the fields, while people went to church to pray and listen to her father's sermons.

Willful and spoiled, Susannah caused much grief to Mister Kingsley. She hated housekeeping, enjoyed hunting and horseback riding, and participated in amateur plays and photography outings with other young English men and women. She mocked Aunt Florence's philanthropy and said terrible things. Her father shuddered when she stated that of all philosophers she preferred Charaka – a coarse materialist who proved that soul and body were one and the same. She hated India and dreamed of returning to London.

The pastor believed that his daughter's whims were caused by the Indian climate, harmful to the Europeans, and by her age. "All this nonsense will pass as soon as she is married," the pastor told himself.

The mass wasn't over yet, but people were pouring from the church doors, shouting and waving their arms.

Was there a fire?

Susannah spurred her horse and saw the boy Paresh-John, who also lived at the house for "strengthening of his faith", which, apparently, required doing all the dirty work to develop the Christian spirit of obedience and humility.

"Hey, Gypsy!" Susannah shouted, reining in her horse, as if calling a dog.

She did not believe that "this monkey" deserved the name of John, like the sahibs, and called the boy "Gypsy". She called all Indians Gypsies, and when her father objected, she replied, "Read *People Science* by Ratzel."

John ran up to Susannah.

"What is going on there?" she asked, pointed at the church with her whip.

"Ah, Miss! There are, Miss, such things, Miss, that..."

Susannah impatiently flicked her whip right over John's head.

"Ben... Binoy, Miss, jumped into the air, Miss, and everyone got scared," the boy blurted out.

"Don't talk nonsense!"

"It's true, Miss! Like this..." and John started jumping. "It was very clever, the way he did it. It was like he was standing on an invisible bench!" John jumped again, trying to stay as far as possible from Susannah's whip.

The pastor stepped out, leaning onto the church groundskeeper.

"Father! What happened?" Susannah asked, alarmed. He loved her father even though, in her heart, she was somewhat annoyed by the weakness of his character.

The pastor walked silently toward home, and she rode next to him, tapping the horse's neck with the whip.

"Tell me!"

"Later, my child," the pastor replied weakly. "I need to... recover a bit."

"The best way to find out what happens in church is to go to church," the groundskeeper mumbled, glancing sullenly at the horse's tail, cut short after the European fashion.

Susannah flicked her whip and shouted, "Gypsy, come here, little demon!"

She hopped off the horse.

John, who really did look like a little Gypsy, ran out of the kitchen with a rag in his hand.

"Take the horse to the stables," the girl ordered, brushing out the pleats in her riding habit.

"Here you are, Aunt Florence! I'll finally find out what is going on. Are you crying, Auntie? What is the matter?"

"It's from happiness, Susie. God blessed me to see a miracle."

"A miracle?" Susannah mocked. "Binoy's jumping is a miracle?"

Her aunt frowned and even paled a little.

"Don't say that! God will punish you! You didn't see it. Ben is a great saint! He wasn't jumping, but rose into the air. Everyone saw it. God made a miracle for his great faith."

"I have always expected something of this sort from you!" Susannah said with a sigh. "Aunt Florence is becoming fanatical, and it won't end well, I've often thought."

"Blasphemer!" the spinster exclaimed indignantly and added meekly, "Judge not and be not judged. May God forgive you and me in His mercy!" and she walked into the house.

Susannah stood in the middle of the garden path thoughtfully. A crowd was approaching the house.

"Saint! *Saniasi*! Bless me! Bless my son! Let me touch your feet!" people in the crowd exclaimed.

The peasants stopped about ten feet from the garden fence, not daring to approach the house. Ben-Ariel stepped out from the crowd. The peasants bowed to him and went back, talking excitedly.

With his head lowered, Ariel entered the garden and walked toward the porch.

"Listen, Binoy, Ben, or whatever your name is..." Susannah stopped him.

Ariel waited.

"What sort of trick did you do in church?"

"*Babu*... Mister Kingsley said that if one really believed, then nothing was impossible. Such is the power of Christian

God. I appealed to the Lord to help me rise above the floor and God listened to me. That is all."

"And God Himself lifted you? Under your arms or by the hair?"

Ariel said nothing. Susannah paused, then chuckled and yelled, her nostrils flaring, "Nonsense! I don't believe it! Do it for me, if you don't want me to call you a liar!"

Ariel sighed, looked at the garden gate, then at the flower bed with carnations and lightly stepped onto one of the flowers. The flower didn't even bend. He crossed the flower bed in this fashion and landed on the path, giving Susannah a humble glance.

"An amusing trick," Susannah said, trying to hide her confusion. "Don't imagine that you have convinced me of your miraculous gift."

"I only did what you asked of me," Ariel replied gently.

"Yes, excellent! And how do you plan to use this ability?"

"God will show me the way."

Susannah stomped her foot.

"I can't stand hypocrisy!" she exclaimed, and then continued thoughtfully, "Let's assume that you can really do this, that this is not hypnosis. What next? Are you going to just do these tricks to plunge old ladies into hysterics in church or to impress the village girls by fluttering over flowers like a butterfly? Or, perhaps, you are planning to work for small change at country fairs? A man should do a real man's job. If I were you, I would become a fireman. Yes, a fireman! I would save people from burning buildings by flying up to the top floors, where their ladders can't reach. Or I would go to work as a lifeguard, instead of pretending to be a saint and living in obscurity, while eating someone else's bread."

"Perhaps, that is what I shall do," Ariel replied, bowed, and went into the house.

"Cunning scoundrel!" Susannah thought, gazing pensively at the flowers.

CHAPTER THIRTY-FOUR. OBSESSION

Having come home, the pastor paced around his study for a long time, running into the light "travel" chairs and small bamboo tables. Like many Englishmen in India, he did not purchase any substantial furniture, believing his stay here to be temporary and brief. In the meantime, years passed since his arrival.

Kingsley was extremely agitated. He clasped his hands so hard that his knuckles crunched and grabbed at his head.

What happened? Was it a miracle? Was it one of those miracles, of which he pontificated so much and so eloquently in his sermons? "There is God!" he remembered someone's exclamation in church. But it was impossible! His practical mind of the 20th century Englishman revolted against miracles.

But if he did not believe in the possibility of a miracle, did that mean he did not believe in God either? The sudden thought shocked him.

He knew that religion was necessary. He was one of the officials, diligently doing his job. Simple folk had a hard time coping with life? It was his duty to support their faith. And here was this boy Ben, who came out of nowhere and turned everything upside down, putting him, the pastor, in a most awkward position. Of course, Ben could not make him believe in the miracle of God, the miracle of the Creator. But then, what was the meaning of this supernatural phenomenon? How was it to be interpreted? What to do next?

It was very enticing to use Ben. But that was a risky game, in which he could compromise himself, the missionary work, and his country and people. Ah, it would be so excellent if he could take advantage of this. He could convert so many pagans and present such a glorious report!

As the pastor walked across his study for the hundredth time, the blessed Aunt Florence stood in Ariel's room with prayerfully folded hands and said, "Can you move mountains too? Please, dear Ben, make that miracle! Do you see that mountain?" she nodded at the window. "Please move it off to the side. Because of it, I never get any sunlight in my room."

"It could kill people and animals living on the mountains and in its vicinity," Ariel replied evasively.

Aunt Florence thought about it. She was overcome with desire for another miracle.

"Well, at least move this table! Or could you make me young again? Or transport me back to England? Make this faded flower bloom again. Or, at the very least cure me from the kidney stones."

"You must not tempt the Lord in vain," Ariel replied, becoming tired of Aunt Florence's persistence.

"What do you mean in vain? Kidney stones cause me terrible pain, and I am terrified of surgery."

"Perhaps, God is punishing you with kidney stones!"

Florence paused, trying to recall, for what sins God might have punished her with kidney stones. Miracle makers were such cantankerous people. Should she offer him a gift? That would offend him – he would accuse her of bargaining for miracles. If only she could procure that proverbial mustard seed's worth of faith!

"Listen, Ben, don't be angry. Perhaps you could transfer some of your faith over to me? At least as small as a speck of dust?"

"It depends on you. Believe, and you shall receive by the strength of your faith!"

Aunt Florence pressed her eyes shut, clenched her fists, and turned red with strain.

"I believe that I shall rise into the air! I believe, Lord, I believe!" she rose on tiptoe. "I think it's happening! Oh, God, really? How frightening! I am rising! I believe, I believe, I believe!" She kept her eyes closed.

Having completely lost his patience, Ariel grabbed Aunt Florence, put her on top of the armoire and ran out of the room. On the stairs, he nearly ran into the pastor.

"Come with me, Ben!"

The pastor took Ariel to his study, made him sit in an armchair and paced around the room.

He finally said, "Listen, Ben, how did you do it?"

"I was bound by my faith," the youth replied modestly.

The pastor wanted to lose his temper but restrained himself.

"Show me your feet!" he ordered.

Kingsley leaned forward and examined his feet. They were ordinary feet. There were no springs or contraptions attached to the soles.

"Were you taught to levitate by the fakirs by any chance?" he asked, even though he had always stated that levitation was nothing but gossip by idle tourists. But now it was easier for him to believe in the tricks performed by fakirs – as long as they were only tricks – than in a miracle performed by the Christian God.

"I don't know what levitation is," Ariel replied simply.

"Very well. If you are deceiving me, then you are deceiving God Himself, and He shall punish you with leprosy. But if you are telling the truth, do you wish to serve Him?"

"All my life belongs to God who makes miracles," Ariel replied.

"Very well. You may go, Ben."

When Ariel left, the pastor said, "The dice are rolling. Whatever happens, happens! This is the best way. I shall use Ben, regardless of what he is, convert a mass of pagans to Christianity, present a splendid report and return to England with the reputation of a great missionary. My successor may sort things out here any way he wishes!"

He imagined awards, a parish in the capitol, perhaps even promotion to a bishop.

Susannah ran into the study, waving a newspaper.

"I told you, father, that your Ben was a swindler. Look, the papers are writing about a flying man. It has to be him."

"But he does fly, does he not?"

"So do pilots and bugs, but they do not present themselves as saints!"

"Listen, Susannah! If you want to go back to London, do not show the newspapers to anyone, do not talk to anyone about Ben, and do not interfere. I am begging you. This will only last a few days, and after that, I promise, we will go back to England for good!"

Ariel did not find Auntie Florence on his armoire. Having summoned her faith, she tried to smoothly descend from the armoire but fell down, bruised her knees, reproached herself for insufficient faith, and returned to her somewhat dark room. The news of the miracle in church spread through the entire area. One would think that Ariel drove people mad.

Aunt Florence either kept jumping up and down with her eyes closed or stared savagely at kitchen pots or scissors and hissed, "Rise! Rise! I believe!"

John hopped around the kitchen, trying in vain to rise into the air and exclaiming, "I believe! Hop! Too little faith. More! I believe! Hop! More! More faith! I believe! Hop!"

In the surrounding villages, people jumped off roofs, tried walking on water, screamed fanatically, "I believe!" and promptly fell or got stuck in the silt.

Alas, not a single one had acquired even a mustard seed's worth of faith. Either that, or the omnipotence of faith was a deception, and some of the victims were already complaining about it.

There was no time to lose. The pastor posted an announcement on the church door, inviting everyone to a mass to celebrate the miracle.

CHAPTER THIRTY-FIVE. TALKING BUSINESS

Pastor Kingsley was overjoyed. The success of the miracle surpassed all his expectations. He served mass every day, and the small church could not accommodate everyone who came to listen. The pastor delivered eloquent sermons about the power of faith and the might of the Christian God, who instantly appeared superior to all the pagan gods.

He was converting people to Christianity by dozens and hundreds. His report was looking more and more promising.

It was true that his congregation only half-paid attention to the sermons. During each service, they waited impatiently for the saint to appear. Ariel performed before the stunned audience after every sermon.

The new converts pestered the pastor with questions as to how to "acquire" the kind of faith that would produce miracles as quickly as possible and why Ben was the only one capable of flying so far? The pastor explained to the best of his ability, encouraged patience, gave advice, and even put together a kind of manual for strengthening one's faith.

People mumbled the quickly memorized prayers, whose meaning they did not comprehend and dreamed of the miracles they would perform when they finally came to possess the required faith. To be honest, most of them did not dream of moving mountains or stopping the sun in its track, but of a new house, a new sari, a buffalo and a donkey, a bowl of rice every day, a cure for an illness. None of them bothered with the kingdom of heaven.

The miraculous demonstrations, which had to be conducted outside of the church due to high demand, were now being attended by Europeans, the local sahibs at first, and then visitors from afar.

The pastor noticed two of them speaking with an American accent, and was struck by the exceptional interest they showed in Ben. "They must be reporters. They might ruin the whole thing," Pastor Kingsley thought with some concern. His worries were not without reason.

One day, the two Americans approached Ariel. Paying no attention to the noisy crowd that surrounded him, one of them said to Ariel in English, "Would you be so kind, Mister, to give us a few minutes of your time for a business discussion?"

Much to the pastor's surprise, Ben quickly replied in perfect English, "I am at your service, gentlemen!" He walked out of the crowd and went with them to a beautiful brand-new car waiting by the side of the road.

Pastor saw the three of them get in the car, but they didn't drive away but spent some time talking.

When they finished, Ariel said good bye and left the car.

"Who were you talking to?" the pastor asked Ariel when they returned home.

"With two visiting gentlemen."

"I saw that. What did you talk about?"

"They are interested in me," Ariel replied. "I must soon leave you, Mister Kingsley. I would like to thank you for the shelter and for all your kindness."

The pastor thought about it. His main objective has been accomplished, and he too was leaving soon. It was just as well that Ben would leave before that.

"Very well, Ben, you are a free man and may do as you please. When do you intend to leave?"

"Tomorrow. If you think it necessary, I can perform the miracle one last time."

"Excellent, my boy," the pastor said gently and rushed to tell the good news to his daughter.

"Ben is leaving."

"Father, must you always say things that upset me?"

Her father looked at her in dismay and thought, "A woman always remains a riddle to a man, even if she is your own daughter."

CHAPTER THIRTY-SIX. FLIGHT

For a worthy conclusion of his missionary activities in India, Pastor Kingsley decided, with Ben's assistance, to stage the last "gala performance" – the rising of a saint into heaven, akin to Saint Enoch who was taken up while still alive.

This was meant to produce extraordinary religious impact and, in addition, provide the best way for Ben to depart.

His bulging missionary report was accompanied by lists including enormous numbers of converts to Christianity. The bishop would be pleased and generously reward Kingsley's apostolic activities. The pastor rubbed his hands, anticipating success. Ben gladly agreed with his plan, and everything was expected to go off splendidly. The saint would go to heaven, and the pastor would pack his suitcases and go to England the same day.

On the day appointed for ascension, many peasants and people from nearby towns came to the large clearing in front of the church early in the morning to get the best view of the miracle. Even the shepherds herded their flocks to the grove and prepared to watch the unusual spectacle. There were several rows of chairs for the local sahibs.

By ten in the morning, the church was surrounded by a veritable crowd. Many came from afar on their oxen, horses, and donkeys. People were standing on their carts, and little kids hung from the trees like bunches of grapes.

Aunt Florence made Ben a long robe, similar to the one in the paintings of Christ, and Susannah – who could have thought! – wove him a wreath of dark-crimson carnations.

So attired, Ariel appeared before the crowd. He looked very impressive.

The greetings from the crowd and the sign from the pastor, who stood on a specially built podium, were followed by reverent silence. Solemn sounds of the organ sounded from the open doors and windows of the church. When the organ finished playing, the pastor began a speech, but the crowd was anxious and clearly could not wait for it to end. Kingsley had to shorten his sermon.

Ariel walked into the middle of the green lawn, smiled, lifted his arms, and started rising slowly. A light breeze moved the hem of his long robe and strands of his long hair. It was a breathtaking sight.

For a few seconds, the crowd watched Ariel silently, as if bewitched, but then it moved and became noisy. People fell to their knees and shouted ecstatically, reaching up, "Lord, why must you leave us?" They already considered him a Messiah. Mothers lifted their children and shouted, "Bless him, Lord!"

Having reached the top of the bell tower, Ariel halted in the air and waved his arms, inviting the crowd to be silent. Once the noise faded, he said loudly, "Hello! Hello! The Chatfield circus is the best in America and in the whole world! Hello! Performances begin in the nearby city! Buy your tickets without delay and you will see far greater wonders!"

Ariel threw the wreath into the crowd, at the feet of the completely confused Aunt Florence, then soared into the air, flew over the steeple, and vanished beyond the grove.

His departure was soon followed by a loud honking of a car horn. A frightened donkey roared, "Hee-haw! Hee-haw! Hee-haw!" and was soon joined by the other donkeys.

They seemed to laugh at the swindled Pastor Kingsley.

CHAPTER THIRTY-SEVEN. HEAVENLY CONTRACTOR

Ariel did not see what happened next, but it wasn't difficult to guess the consequences. This was a complete fiasco of Pastor Kingsley's missionary activity, most likely to be followed by an exile to a minor parish somewhere in the heart of provincial England.

The son of the director of the American circus, James Chatfield, and the director of traveling circuses Edwin Grigg came to India with a dozen mobile shapito circuses. Chatfield and Grigg were in charge of the tour but also made time to study the "local market". Their main goal was to find and hire performers from India to come to America. The public required more and more novelty, and the European riders, gymnasts, contortionists, and magicians were not much different from the American ones. Something exotic could be successfully used. In every town or even a small village they traveled through, Chatfield and Grigg visited markets, fairs, and folk celebrations and explored the local spectacles, acrobats, snake charmers, singers, musicians, fakirs, and illusionists, selecting the best for their circus.

The Indians weren't too anxious to leave their homeland and go on a long journey, but Grigg showed them handfuls of American dollars, offered advances, promised great earnings and, thus, had assembled a sizeable exotic troupe.

He and Chatfield were already working on a captivating spectacle *Mysteries of India*, with gorgeous sets, monkeys, parrots, oxen, elephants, crocodiles, and fakirs.

One day, Chatfield ran into an article in a local English newspaper, titled *Who is he, after all?* The article talked about the mysterious flying man who appeared from time to time in various places and then vanished without a trace.

Chatfield read the article and handed it to Grigg with a laugh, "Here they are, Mister Grigg, the miracles of India! The nonsense some papers publish these days! Apparently, the Indian audience is even more gullible and stupid than the American one. I don't know a single journalist who would have tried to sell this."

Grigg read the article carefully and said, "It would be nice to get this flying man for our circus."

"Indeed!" James Chatfield laughed in earnest.

"I am absolutely serious," Grigg replied. "I have already talked about the flying man to some of the Indians we hired. They assure me that he is not a fantasy."

"But of course, not one of them has ever seen him, have they?"

"The snake charmer... I can't remember his name, assured me that he saw the flying man with his own eyes, when he snatched some little boy in the middle of a fair and flew away with him."

Chatfield shook his head doubtfully.

But he was soon forced to believe in the existence of the flying man. As their tour continued, they met more and more people who swore they saw the flying man and even provided directions to the area where he lived. Chatfield became honestly interested and changed their travel route to find the flying man.

That was how Chatfield and Grigg met with Ariel by the church and had a brief conversation with him, at first, and a more substantial one later.

The practical Americans were not at all interested in who Ariel was, how he flew, and what his past was.

Even if Ariel said, "I am a spirit. I am an angel," James Chatfield, not in the least surprised, would have replied, "All right! I would like to offer you a contract. What are your terms?"

Chatfield used that kind of businesslike briefness when he spoke to Ariel.

"Mister... mister?"

"Ben," Ariel replied.

"All right, Mister Ben. We are interested in your ability to fly. Come to work for us. You will fly in America and receive very good compensation for it."

Ariel knew that America was very far away from India. With the ocean between the two countries, he would be safe. He had to accept this job of his own free will, and then return for his friends. Fate herself was favoring him.

He agreed without further ado.

Mister Chatfield was puzzled by his answer. Were they really dealing with an angel? He agreed without haggling, without even asking how much they were going to pay him!

Did he not understand that he was *sans pair*, as the French said? That he had no equal and could ask for any sum? If he wasn't an angel or an idiot, he could have been a criminal who tried to escape across the ocean, which he, apparently, couldn't cross on his own. Grigg did mention the kidnapping of the little boy. Did it matter? The main thing was that the man was a golden goose.

Grigg, who was older and more experienced, figured out Ariel's true nature sooner – this young man simply had no experience in life and no idea of his own worth.

"We shall talk about the terms later," Grigg interrupted, worried that the director's son might get Ariel too fixated on his own uniqueness. "I am sure we can agree on the amount."

"It's just that I wanted…"

Chatfield and Grigg perked up.

"What did you want?"

"Before we sail across the ocean, I wanted to visit two places. I need to see my friends and… one other person. It is possible that I will need your assistance."

"Of course, naturally, we are at your service, Mister Ben. Anything we can do!"

"What say you, Mister Grigg?" Chatfield asked, once they were alone.

"I say we found a treasure, Mister Chatfield. India is truly the land of wonders."

"We should think about advertising," James noted.

Publicity was his favorite part of the business.

"That pastor was in the wrong line of work. He should have been a circus director. He came up with a great number. Why can't we use the ascension for our campaign? We could discuss it with Ben. He can play for the pastor up to the height of fifty meters, and for us – higher than that. After all, we bought Ben! He will sing praises to our circus from above."

Grigg disagreed, finding this idea impractical and even distasteful. The stubborn James insisted, and Grigg had to give in.

The wise old Mister Grigg turned out to be right – the heavenly publicity caused them much fuss and many troubles. They had to deal with representatives of the church and English government.

When time came to make another decision, Grigg stood his ground. Chatfield dreamed of showing the flying man in America and wanted to send forward telegrams, declaring the upcoming arrival of the "World-wide phenomenon!"

Grigg, who had grown gray in the circus arena and had excellent knowledge of the audience's psychology, objected heatedly. Of course, the public would go to watch the flying man, just as it went to watch the first airplane flights. And they could make a lot of money with it. But people became used to things very quickly. Who in their day and age would pay to go look at an airplane in flight? The same thing could happen to the flying man! Anyone who saw him once or twice would not want to watch him the third time.

"But we will have enough time to make millions!" James argued.

"Why not make tens of millions?" Grigg retorted.

"How do you plan to do that? How do you plan to use Ben?"

"First of all, forget that he can fly. Do not send any messages about it to America, and do not talk to anyone along the way. Understand, the audience gets tired of everything except one thing – struggle, competition, with its constant changes and questionable outcomes. People spend minutes watching the rarest animals in the world, but are prepared to spend hours watching the stupid cock fights. Passions flare, people become excited, they make bets."

"I think I am beginning to understand you. I believe you are right," Chatfield said after a thought.

"A hundred percent," Grigg replied confidently.

Having discovered the priceless treasure that was Ben, Chatfield and Grigg decided to hand the administrative matters over to one of the oldest managers of their touring circus and leave for America immediately.

When they left the little town in the mountains, leaving the pastor to sort out his own mess, James asked Ariel, where he wanted to go.

Ariel honestly told his story to the Americans. Chatfield was delighted by it and laughed many times.

Grigg thought, "Ben-Aricl must be a victim of someone's intrigues. Who knows, perhaps he is a son of wealthy and prominent parents. We must keep this in mind. Lolita is nothing but a youthful infatuation. Why not stop by and visit that little teenage widow? After all, we can take Lolita, Nizmat, and Sharad with us and put them to work. But Ariel also wants to visit Dandarhat and meet with Piers. I wish we could avoid it. Piers is clearly a dangerous competitor. Of course, we will protect Ariel and won't let Piers lay his hands on him. However, it is still risky. Ariel, who agreed so eagerly to go to America in order to get away from Piers, was now seeking to meet with him. Why? Ariel says it is to discover the mystery of his origins, which Piers must know. Very well! But once he knows where he is from, would he prefer to go back to his family instead of going to America?"

Grigg shared his concerns with Chatfield. This time, Chatfield and Grigg quickly agreed – they had to take every possible measure to keep Ariel from going to Dandarhat and meeting with Piers. If Ariel insisted on it and obtained the information he was looking for, they had to make him promise that he would work at the circus for at least a year.

Only then would they guarantee their help during the meeting with Piers.

Ariel accepted their terms.

CHAPTER THIRTY-EIGHT. "ALL THINGS PASS LIKE A DREAM"

They reached the marble palaces of Raja Rajkumar with their golden roofs in the evening and saw them in all the splendor of the setting sun. Ariel's heart beat faster. He wondered about Shiama's fate. When they passed the palaces, he looked at the balconies and thought he saw Shiama. But it may have been another woman who looked like her. It would have taken him less than a minute to fly from the car to the balcony, but Chatfield made him promise not to fly, and Ariel stayed put.

There was the lake, and the grove, and Nizmat's cabin beyond. Ariel's excitement grew. He wanted even more to fly to his friends.

To give Ariel some privacy, Grigg ordered the driver to stop the car by the mango tree, from which Ariel once picked fruit for Sharad.

Ariel stepped out of the car and saw Sharad and Lolita. Unable to restrain himself any longer, he ran, barely touching the ground with his feet. Grigg watched him and said to Chatfield, "Look at him run! We'll make him into a world-class runner."

Lolita and Sharad were sitting on the porch steps and rose at the sight of the approaching sahib. They didn't recognize Ariel. Suddenly, Sharad shouted, "*Dada!*" and ran to his friend, but then halted and shied away. Ariel was wearing an excellent European suit and a broad-brimmed hat. His hair was cut short.

"What is it?" Ariel exclaimed with a laugh, then hugged and kissed the boy who clutched at his hand.

Lolita, having also recognized Ariel, performed *pronam*[viii] with a formal bow. Once again, Ariel was faced with the wall of reverence. He wanted to embrace Lolita, tell her that he loved her and ask her to be his wife. But her formal bow made him feel awkward and tongue-tied.

"Hello, Lolita! See, I did as I promised!" he said, walking up to the girl. "I came back. Where is Nizmat?"

"He is very ill," Lolita replied, nevertheless looking at Ariel in delight.

Ariel quickly entered the cabin. In the dim light, he saw Nizmat lying on a mat. Ariel greeted the old man, whose eyes flashed with joy.

"Master! Is it you? Lolita was right! You couldn't have died. And you came back to us. Thank you!" he said with difficulty. "I am dying."

"You will not die, Nizmat!" Ariel objected, taking the old man's emaciated hand.

"All living things must die," he replied calmly. "Dry flowers must not sadden one's eyes, and so they are burned."

Ariel tried to console the old man. No, Nizmat would recover soon. Ariel would send a doctor and Nizmat would get better and join him in America, along with Lolita and Sharad. Ariel told him that he loved Lolita and wanted to marry her.

Nizmat listened with his eyes closed, moving his hands in front of him, as if pushing something away. Then he spoke. He thanked Ariel for the honor. Lolita's fate worried him greatly. She said she would never marry. Blind Tara said she would curse her son if he married Lolita. But Lolita rejected Ishvar before that, and Ishvar left for the city and never came back. What would happen to Lolita after Nizmat's death? But a poor girl was no match for gods, demigods, and sahibs.

"Krishna himself would have been glad to have such a wife!" Ariel objected passionately.

Nizmat smiled weakly, opened his eyes and, glancing at Ariel, asked, "But would the wife be happy in such an uneven match?"

Ariel was taken aback, but then tried proving to Nizmat the possibility of such a match.

He knew he could not take Lolita with him right away. He could not leave Nizmat alone or with only Sharad to care for him.

"We will talk about it later," Ariel said sadly and stepped out onto the porch.

"Lolita!" Ariel said, taking her hand. "I will send a doctor, and grandpa will get better. Just don't call the village healer. He will kill Nizmat like he killed his son. I must leave, but I will come back, Lolita. I will take you with me. When grandpa gets well, I want you to marry me."

He didn't take his eyes off Lolita's pale face. It was beautiful but expressed more suffering and fear than joy, which caused Ariel acute pain. He wanted so much to make this girl happy.

"Won't you say something, Lolita?"

"I do not know what to say, my lord."

"But... do you love me?"

The girl stood with her eyes downcast. Her hand shook in Ariel's.

"She waited for you the entire time, she only spoke about you!" Sharad shouted. "And we'll go! All of us together!"

"Wait a minute, I'll be right back!" Ariel said and quickly walked to the car.

"Pardon me, sirs, I believe you promised me some money?" he said awkwardly. "My friend, the old Nizmat, is very ill, he needs a doctor and some medicine."

Grigg gladly gave Ariel several large bills and reminded him that they had to be going. Grigg was not worried about money at the moment. The main thing was to take Ariel away. While the sum he provided was substantial to a poor Indian family, on the scale of an American circus company it was nothing.

Ariel took the money, feeling sincerely grateful.

"I am such an idiot," he thought when he returned. "I should have asked for some money earlier and bought some presents. A new pipe and good tobacco for Nizmat, a scarf and bracelets for Lolita, and maybe a new shirt for Sharad. They would have been so happy! But I will send them some things later."

"Here, Nizmat, take this money," he said returning to the old man. "Promise me you will get a doctor. And eat well. I will send you more money. Get well soon. Good bye, Nizmat!"

"Thank you. Farewell!" Nizmat replied.

On the porch, Ariel walked up to Lolita and kissed her forehead.

"Good bye, my Lolita! Take care of grandfather and Sharad. I will send you money and packages, and many letters, and then I will come back for you."

As if delirious, Lolita said, looking off into space, "I will wait for you, but dreams pass. All things pass like a dream. Maia!"

Ariel looked at her in surprise, then smiled and said, "This will not pass like a dream, darling! Wait for me!"

"Take me with you, *dada*!" Sharad pleaded, hugging him.

"I would love for you to come with me, Sharad. But Lolita would have a hard time all by herself, what with grandpa sick."

"Yes, that's true," Sharad sighed. "We have to wait for grandpa to get better, and then we will go stay with you."

"I will come for you myself."

Ariel returned to the car slowly and with heavy heart.

The car beeped and took off.

Ariel rode deeply in thought. Why did he leave them? Why did he have to go to the strange, distant America? What waited for him there? Would it not have been better to stay? But then he would once again become the helpless flying man, the plaything of fates, and sport for evil people. He would only come to harm and hurt Lolita as well. No, he was doing the right thing! First he must win his freedom, get on his feet, find out who he was, and then join his friends to never be parted again.

He could still hear Lolita's mysterious words, "Dreams pass. All things pass like a dream. Maia!"

CHAPTER THIRTY-NINE. "ELEVATED" CONVERSATION

Piers and his entire theosophical society were beginning to harden themselves to the idea that Ariel was lost to them. The flying man caused one more sensation – "Pastor Kingsley's miracle", which, according to the newspapers, turned out to be a clever publicity stunt by an American circus. After that, Ariel vanished, apparently captured by the Americans. Piers realized the difficulty involved in getting him away from them. Ariel's guardian, Boden, could have done it. Piers had written to London to inform Boden and Heslon about the situation.

"If we hear about the flying man," Piers wrote, "it would most likely come from the United States of America, where you should direct your search." Having dispatched the letter, Piers was walking across the Dandarhat courtyard back to his study in his cat-like gait.

The sky was clear, the sun was barely above the horizon, but the air was already heating up. The last breath of the cool morning breeze was fading away. As usual, the courtyard and the buildings were silent. Only the gravel crunched under his feet.

Piers' sensitive ear caught someone else's footsteps from the direction of the gates. He quickly turned to look and saw Ariel. The boy was very grown-up and dressed in a handsome white suit.

Piers was dumbstruck. He was glad but also cautious. The young man was walking toward him with way too much confidence.

He was followed by two gentlemen.

One word from Piers, and tutors, overseers, and servants would run to his aid. And so he made a pleasantly astonished face, as if he only just recognized Ariel, and rushed to meet him with outstretched arms.

"I am glad to see you, Ariel! You did well to come back on your own!" He firmly wrapped his right hand around Ariel's left wrist. He wanted to clasp the other hand as well, but Ariel anticipated and grabbed Piers' left wrist. They stood, clutching each other and looking into each other's eyes, as if trying to guess the other's intentions.

"Damn it! Who caught whom?" Piers thought anxiously.

The gentlemen following Ariel stopped and watched the scene curiously.

"Perhaps, we should go to my study? We would be more comfortable there. Are you hungry, Ariel? Or perhaps you are tired from your trip?" Piers asked, barely maintaining composure.

"Mister Piers!" Ariel said firmly, ignoring his questions. "I came here to find out from you, here and now, about my origins. You must give me the answer immediately."

Suddenly feeling the need to address Ariel more formally, Piers replied, "You were brought to Dandarhat fifteen years ago, sir, by a man I knew nothing about. He did not tell me his name or where you came from. There are many such children at Dandarhat."

Ariel's hand squeezed harder, and Piers felt that the young man lifted him into the air. Piers felt chilled with terror. He wanted the scream, but realized that this would only worsen his situation. Ariel was not alone, perhaps his escorts were bribed assassins. Ariel could take him away and get rid of him at his leisure. Piers clutched harder at Ariel's hand to keep from falling down. His head was level with the young man's chest.

Having lifted Piers into the air, Ariel halted and said, "We can now continue our conversation where we will not be disturbed. Listen to me, Mister Piers!"

Ariel's voice was stern, but somewhat halting – Piers was heavy and required some effort to hold up.

It was easy to say "listen"! Piers' teeth were chattering when he fearfully glanced at the yellow gravel below.

"If you do not tell me the truth about myself, I will let go of your right hand and spin you in the air, until you break free and crash. Or would you like to wrestle me here, in the air?"

"I will tell... I will tell the truth," Piers wheezed, having lost his voice from anxiety.

Ariel flew up to the astonished Chatfield and Grigg and landed next to them, breathing heavily, "Mister Grigg... please... write down this man's testimony!"

Grigg pulled out a notepad and a pen, and Piers, still hoarse from the ordeal, told everything he knew about Ariel. He also provided addresses of Boden and Jane Galton.

Ariel let go of Piers' hand and said dryly, "You may go. But remember, if you gave false information…"

"It is absolutely accurate!" Piers exclaimed. He slumped and his legs shook under him, as he ran across the courtyard to his study.

"Well, sir, we have fulfilled our promise. We hope that you will now fulfill yours," James said, giving Ariel a searching look.

"I shall. We are going to America," Ariel replied. "My sister can come to me there. I will write to her."

They returned to the car.

CHAPTER FORTY. "BINOY THE UNDEFEATED"

Chatfield Senior was very pleased with the Indian find. The head of the company approved Grigg's plan.

Not a single person in America was supposed to know that Binoy-Ben-Ariel-Aurelius Galton could fly. Of course, the rumors about him had already reached across the Atlantic, but the articles were generally laughed off as scams. No one knew what Ariel looked like.

Chatfield explained to Ariel what his role was going to be – he was not supposed to give any indication that he could fly, but he was to use his unusual gift to beat all the world records in running, swimming, obstacle courses and gymnastics.

Ariel's tutelage supervised by Grigg and both Chatfields lasted for some time. Of course, Ariel had no trouble jumping over the obstacles of any height or flying from one trapeze to another across the entire circus arena.

The complexity was, as Grigg said, in "not breaking boundaries of what was physically possible for a human being." He had to work in a way that the public would see something astounding, but not impossible. They had to be very careful. For example, during the high jump, Ariel had to curb his leaps to only surpass the world records by a few centimeters.

When it came to running, the Chatfields and Grigg trained Ariel with the best runners in a deserted area.

Ariel was introduced to various schools of running and taught all the traits of an experienced runner. In the presence of others he was expected to imitate fatigue and shortness of breath.

To sustain the audience's interest, he had to pretend in some competitions that he was losing energy, allow his competitors to get ahead of him, but then beat him to the finish line at the last moment. In other words, he had to act like an experienced gambler, who never showed all his advantages to the fullest.

His circus performances were prepared in a separate mobile tent. Chatfield Junior was particularly interested in horse numbers – gymnastics at full gallop and somersaults. Of course, Ariel could do real miracles, and the old Grigg, much to the disappointment of the young Chatfield, had to constantly hold him back. "It's too much! Don't do quadruple somersaults!" he interrupted angrily.

While the training took place, Chatfield Junior, betting on the returns, spared no money on an advertising campaign of unprecedented scale, even for America.

Before they ever saw Binoy – "The wonder of the world discovered in the jungle of mysterious India" – people already knew about him. From the portraits in the newspapers, magazines, billboards, and posters, Americans had learned Ariel's features better than those of the President.

He already had obsessive fans who tried every trick in the book to see him. Experienced gamblers were already making bets. Reporters flooded the press with sensational announcements about the upcoming performances of the "Undefeated".

Ariel received the title of "Binoy the Undefeated" in advance, before a single performance took place. But he earned it right away, as soon as he began his triumphant tour.

Ariel defeated one world champion after another. The most amazing part was that he set new world records in various kinds of sports. His fans literally carried him around on their shoulders, and he made certain to give his body normal weight on those occasions.

A game that could not be lost had its risks. Gamblers who lost repeatedly grumbled and mentioned clever trickery. Fewer and fewer people bet against Ariel, because without any variety, the game was losing its zest.

The Chatfields and Grigg decided that the time was right for the old, reliable circus trick to renew the interest in the competitions – Binoy had to "suffer" a few losses, followed, of course, by the even more glorious victories.

Time passed.

Ariel had traveled to almost every large city in America. The Chatfield Company profits were unprecedented in the circus history.

The more successful they were, the more carefully Chatfield Senior watched Ariel and thought, "Any moment now he will bring up an increase in his pay."

But he was mistaken, thinking that Ariel would become infected by the spirit of profit.

As soon as he started making big money, packages and money orders began streaming from America to the remote corner of India. This time, nothing was forgotten – scarves and bracelets for Lolita, shirts for Sharad, pipes and tobacco for Nizmat. Despite all his triumphs, Ariel never forgot his friends. From time to time he received letters from them, filled with love and gratitude. Nizmat was feeling better. Everyone was waiting for him. Many times, Ariel was ready to drop everything and fly to the cabin by the mango trees. He also helped the poor circus staff. Fame and money gave Ariel the ability to fully apply his genuine human kindness.

CHAPTER FORTY-ONE. TWO WORLDS

One time, having just triumphed in one of the most complicated parts of the program, Ariel was bowing to the wildly applauding audience and noticed with some surprise a girl who was watching him. She was in a box nearest to the arena and observed him with a sad expression, her hands folded on the barrier. The girl's face seemed familiar. Yes, she was the same girl he glimpsed during his illness, when he was captured by Piers. So, that was his sister!

Was it really his sister Jane? He did send her a telegram when he arrived in America.

Having bowed countless times, Ariel anxiously returned to his dressing room.

Was he mistaken? He started changing out of his costume.

An usher came in with a calling card that read "Lady Jane Galton. London". Below was a note, penciled in a sharp, confident, almost manly cursive, "Will wait by the exit. J.G."

A vague memory flickered through Ariel's mind, "Jane Galton. Yes, she is indeed my sister!"

Ariel quickly finished changing and left. It took him some time to make his way through the mass of cars surrounding the circus. Someone in the crowd recognized him and started applauding. Ariel looked around, at a loss, and bowed out of habit.

There she was!

He walked up to Jane, not knowing how to greet her.

Jane held out her hand formally, as if wanting to prevent any expression of brotherly sentiments. Ariel awkwardly shook her slender hand, encased in a brown kidskin glove. He noticed that his sister was frowning.

"The car will be along shortly," she said.

He guessed rather than heard her words through all the noise.

They hurried toward the car.

As soon as they made their way from the solid flood of other cars, Jane turned toward Ariel, smiled slightly, and asked, "Did you recognize me, Aurelius?"

"Yes, of course, Jane. You were so close there, in India. If only I knew!" He took her hand, but Jane immediately pulled it away and said quickly, "We will discuss everything at the hotel!"

When they entered her hotel suite, Jane took her brother's hand and looked at him sadly. She then kissed his forehead.

"Finally, I have found you, Aurelius!" she said quietly.

"And I found you," Ariel replied, not daring to hug or kiss her.

They sat down.

"I didn't write to you because I wanted to get all the information first. I have been deceived so many times. But I have no doubt that you are my brother. Here, let me show you the portrait of our parents."

She opened a box and held out a photo.

He saw a young woman with sad eyes and next to her a smiling stocky man in a tuxedo, with a medal on his chest.

Ariel couldn't help himself and exclaimed, "Will I really become like our father?"

"It would be very bad if you do not become like him," Jane said reproachfully.

"But the wrinkles, and the belly…"

"Old age is never kind. Our father was the worthiest of men, Aurelius!" Jane said instructively. "That is what I mean when I say you must become like him. Our father was never referred to in any way other than 'pillar of society'. The noble blood of one of the best families in England flowed through his veins, he was a respected citizen, a good Christian, and the best landlord. He left a large fortune, sadly rather diminished by the guardians Boden and Heslon, according to Mister Dotaller."

Ariel was beginning to understand where Jane was going.

"Well then… We are of noble blood. I can't think of anything I've done that is regrettable."

Jane sighed.

"I am not blaming you. But there are many things that sadden me. What would our father, Sir Thomas Galton, say if he found out that his son was a circus gymnast?"

Ariel became flushed.

"But, Jane, you know how it happened. And, besides, I find nothing shameful about my work. It's honest work and I earn good money."

"Of course, circus performers are nowhere near as bad as muggers and counterfeiters," Jane said with vexation, "but what is suitable for the dregs of society is not suitable for the son of a lord."

Not giving Ariel an opportunity to object, she continued, "And what about your flying? You don't fly now, but I know the secret of your successes. I saw you fly away from us that time in India. A flying man is like an insect or a bird. This violates all Christian and human laws, and for us it is simply indecent, Aurelius! A flying lord – it's incomprehensible! It's shocking! It's disgusting! It's impossible to describe."

"But people fly in airplanes!" Ariel wanted to object, the way he once told Lolita. But Lolita considered him a demigod, whereas Jane considered his ability disdainful and humiliating.

"I know what you will say, Aurelius," Jane continued quickly. "Of course, it is not your fault that you were made into a flying freak. But mistakes – your own and those of the others – must be corrected. Fortunately, no one in England knows anything about you, everyone thinks you are studying at Oxford, so we can take care of it all. But you must forever, do you hear me, forever forget about your flights, if this ability cannot be eliminated through some sort of surgery. I made inquiries with Mister Piers. Unfortunately, that mad scientist who made you into the flying man… What was his name?"

"Mister Hyde."

"Yes. This Hyde is no longer around. Something happened to him. I think he tried becoming a flying man himself, did something wrong, jumped up to the ceiling and crushed his head. He had a cerebral hemorrhage and died. A worthy death for the madman!" Jane's voice acquired a mean quality. "It is too risky to consult any other scientists, because this could become public, and besides, it is unlikely that anyone else could help. Which is why the only solution is for you to forget about your... deficiency and never use it, even if a child should drown before your eyes. And one other thing," she continued, barely drawing a breath. "You must immediately annul your contract with the circus, stop leading this gypsy life and come back to England."

"But I made a promise..."

"Family honor is more important than money. I believe that we have enough to pay any fines."

Ariel was silent. He disagreed with Jane. This was not the way he imagined the first meeting with his sister, and this was not the person he imagined Jane to be.

"I believe I must give notice to Mister Chatfield and give a few farewell performances," Ariel started uncertainly.

"Absolutely not! This would be a great mistake. Right now, everyone thinks you are an obscure Indian. But my presence alone might get people to think in a different direction, and then someone will start making inquiries. You know how much the reporters are interested in you, how they watch your every step and keep trying to find out and write something new about you and your past. If they uncover the truth, our lives will be ruined – yours and mine. I will not be able to stand this kind if dishonor to our family, and will have to become a nun. We must leave right away. I have already ordered the tickets. Go get your things and come back to join me. You can inform your circus bosses about your decision once we are on our way, and Mister Dotaller will take care of the rest. He is an amazingly sensible man."

"I am free for the evening, but there is a performance tomorrow, and tickets have been sold out. There is an announcement about it at the ticket booth, as usual," Ariel added with some pride.

"They will have to return the money, that is all! What would they do if you got sick? They have made enough from your performances."

Ariel wished for only one thing – to end this conversation.

"Very well, Jane, I shall join you as soon as I am ready," he said impatiently.

"No later than midnight," Jane replied, glancing at her watch, and added, "The ship sails tomorrow at eight. We still have a little time. I will tell you about our relatives, the circle of my friends who will soon become your friends, about London."

It was late in the evening when Ariel returned to his apartment. He was considering his sister's ultimatum.

CHAPTER FORTY-TWO. A SUFFERING MOTHER

When Ariel arrived to his room, he saw a young, elegantly dressed woman waiting for him by the door.

Her eyes were red from crying and her face was filled with anxiety.

"Mister Binoy!" the woman said in a halting voice. "I have been waiting for you for several hours. I was at your matinee performance and wanted to see you, but you left with a lady. I found out your address at the circus office and came here to wait for you. My God! If you only knew what I have been through! It's been hours, and every minute is precious."

"You have been standing by my door this entire time?" Ariel asked with concern.

He had visitors frequently – usually his fans. But this woman was not like them.

It was clear that she was driven by some deep personal tragedy. But what could he do?

Ariel quickly unlocked the door and invited her in. Still in her expensive fur wrap and hat, the woman suddenly fell to her knees before him.

"You are the only person who can help the unfortunate mother, begging you…"

"Please, get up, Madam. Please! Sit, calm down. What is the matter?"

"I won't get up until you promise to help me in my troubles. I am worn out."

She burst into tears.

"Of course, if it is within my ability, although I am in a hurry, I only have a little time left."

"It won't take long."

Ariel finally managed to raise the woman from her knees and settle her in an armchair. She pulled out a perfumed handkerchief trimmed with lace, pressed it to her eyes and told him her story, sobbing the entire time.

Mister Binoy was a foreigner and, therefore, could not know some of the more frightening aspects of America and the terrible city of New York. Not a single wealthy person could feel safe here. Had he ever heard of gangsters? An American criminal operating on a large scale was far above and beyond a French mugger or an Indian pickpocket. Was Mister Binoy familiar with the name of Al Capone? No? There were many others like Al Capone. The greatest American gangsters were very wealthy. They had mansions, cars, yachts, and large bank accounts. They bribed the police into protecting them. The gangsters carried out their crimes unimpeded, robbed banks, kidnapped millionaires in broad daylight and, what was much worse, kidnapped their children. They demanded a ransom but when they received it, they killed the child nonetheless. The strange thing was, the wealthier the person, the less he could count on the assistance from the police, when it came to the gangsters.

The visitor sighed.

"Forgive me for getting into so much detail," she continued in a moment, "but it is necessary in order for you to understand me and my hopeless situation." She once again pressed the handkerchief to her eyes. "My name is Warrender. My husband and I are one of the wealthiest families in the States. But our biggest treasure is our only son, Sam. He is only three years old. He has been kidnapped. I am afraid he will die a terrible death."

Missus Warrender dissolved into sobs once again. Ariel was shocked by this drama.

"Calm down, Madam. Have a glass of water. What can I do to help you?"

She had a few sips, her teeth chattering against the edge of the glass.

"Thank you. I will explain. The kidnappers have already sent us several letters, demanding a five million dollar ransom. My husband would have paid immediately, but my brother convinced him to wait. When they get the money, they will kill my Sam, my little boy." She shuddered. "Mark, my brother wants to wait, in hopes of finding a way to save him. The police, of course, has been bribed. The Chief of Police told us, 'We are doing everything possible, but unfortunately, we haven't yet tracked down the criminals who kidnapped your son.' Then we, or rather, my brother Mark, because my husband and I have completely lost our minds with grief, hired private detectives, paid them whatever they asked, and they were able to find out a thing or two. For example, they discovered where my son was kept. The police were looking for him, or pretending to look for him, in the slums, in the suburbs, even in the Upstate mountains, while the poor baby has been kept in the heart of the city, on the ninety-third floor of one of the tallest skyscrapers. Who could have thought? Now we get to the point."

Missus Warrender paused, looked at Ariel, and asked an unexpected question, "Mister Binoy, can you fly?"

"Me? Fly? What a strange idea. Why are you asking me that?"

"Because everything depends on your answer. Of course it is a strange thought, an impossible one, in fact. Perhaps you think that I went mad with grief. But it is not my idea. One of the detectives I mentioned, a very observant and intelligent man, told me that he watched you very carefully and that the secret of your athletic successes is your ability to fly."

Ariel was at a loss and didn't know what to say, but the visitor ignored his confusion and continued, "That detective, Mister Tuts, has been watching all your performances, doing some calculations and collecting all the newspaper material he could find about the 'flying man' from India. You are from India, aren't you? And he told us, 'The only man who can save your son is Mister Binoy, if he agrees. You must ask him!' So here I am – to ask you."

She made a movement to fall to her knees again, but Ariel held her back.

"Please, calm down," he almost ordered. "Let me think whether I can help you."

So, there were people in America who knew who he was.

This meant that, soon, his secret would become public knowledge. That would lead to enormous scandals.

The gamblers who bet against him would be outraged! Following this discovery, the secret of his origin would also soon become known, which meant another scandal for Jane. Were the European prejudices any better than the Indian ones? It was true, Jane was not the kind of person he dreamed she would be, but she was still his sister. He had to leave as soon as possible.

But what was he to do about Missus Warrender's request?

Of course, the young mother was hoping that the flying man could pull her child out of the hands of the criminals by flying into the ninety-third story window.

Many people were bound to notice his flight above the city. And, of course, Jane would be outraged at the mere thought. But this was necessary to save a little boy. She didn't have to face the suffering mother – the mother of little Sam!

How could he resist?

Besides, he was unlikely to be recognized, especially so late at night. He could fly at higher altitude at first, and, in any case, he was leaving in the morning.

The only remaining question was, did he have enough time?

"I am prepared to help you, Madam, but unfortunately I have very little time, only two or three hours. I am being called away."

"You won't need more than two hours," Missus Warrender replied quickly and happily. "Our apartment is nearby and almost right next to the one where my poor boy is being kept.

There is a car waiting outside. Do you agree? You won't refuse me?" she asked, looking at Ariel pleadingly.

He nodded, Missus Warrender shook his hand, and they left the hotel together.

CHAPTER FORTY-THREE. ANOTHER LIE

When Ariel and Missus Warrender arrived at the luxurious apartment, they found Tuts, the detective, Missus Warrender's brother Mark and Mister Warrender, the father of the kidnapped boy, waiting for them. The father seemed completely distraught, almost mad. He had an energetic clear-cut face and short hair, graying at the temples. Mister Warrender held out his hand to Ariel, and a painful smile flickered across his face. He gestured for the visitor to sit down.

"Thank you, sir, for responding to our troubles. They will tell you everything," he pointed at Tuts and Mark. "I... I don't have the energy, forgive me."

"Your task is simple, sir," Tuts said, "but you must act swiftly and assertively. Here is the plan of the city and the photograph of the building. These crosses mark the floor, the apartment, and the window. The windows are always open. Here is the plan of the apartment."

Tuts outlined the plan quickly, clearly, and in a very businesslike way.

"If we don't get the child back tonight, tomorrow will be too late. Come, I'll show you where you can take off."

Ariel walked up to the flat roof, where the Warrenders had a garden, and swiftly rose straight up.

He hasn't flown in a long time and happily surrendered to the familiar feeling of freedom, ease, and the expanse of the sky. How could he ever give that up?

Oh, if only he could take Lolita to some wonderful free country with beautiful flowers and trees. Why didn't he take her to his jungle home? They could all live in a tree.

But there was no time for dreaming. The enormous city thundered and roiled beneath. Stars flickered peacefully in the dark blue sky above him. Ariel looked down again. He saw the Island of Manhattan, like an enormous map, divided into squares that were city blocks, with the dark rectangle of Central Park and the long glittering line of Broadway. There was the jagged shoreline with its docks and piers. There was the broad black Hudson, reflecting the lights of countless ships and barges. Long Island... The Statue of Liberty with the eternally burning torch. The light-flooded streets looked like a glowing grid. The skyscrapers rose like gloomy mountains. The work day was over, and most office buildings were dark. Countless office clerks went home. The lower stories of the buildings shone brightly with their store windows and advertisements, casting a reddish glow upon the walls. Some of the dark skyscrapers were encircled with snake-line glowing signs. A handful of still-lit top-floor windows looked like large stars that fell from the sky and didn't quite reach the ground.

In the distance, the black smooth waters of the ocean stretched to the horizon, with its moving beacons of ship lights.

Ariel felt the cool breath of the ocean and happily enjoyed the clean air high above the city.

He had no trouble finding the right skyscraper, floor, and apartment, and headed to his goal – the first window from the corner.

Tuts didn't lie – the window was open and lit.

Ariel looked in. The well-furnished room was empty.

He then flew in and landed.

He had to go through the door straight across, and then to the left. The nursery should be there.

All he had to do was go in, grab the boy, wrap him up against the nighttime chill and fly away.

Should he meet anyone, he was not supposed to say anything, but act quickly, taking advantage of the element of surprise and confusion.

Ariel went to the door on the left and opened it quietly. He saw the nursery. There was the little boy in his crib, and a young woman was leaning over him tenderly. The boy was restless and crying quietly.

"Mommy," he suddenly called and reached up.

The young woman picked up the child and kissed him with all the tenderness of a mother. The boy put his head on her shoulder and wrapped his littler arms around her neck.

"Oh, little one, don't cry, Sam, don't cry sweetheart!"

The woman's back was turned to Ariel.

He stood there in complete confusion, not knowing what to do. There was no doubt that the woman he saw next to the child was his mother. But then, who was Missus Warrender, and which little Sam did she talk about? He could not very well snatch the child from his mother's arms. As she rocked the boy, the woman turned and noticed Ariel. She smiled and walked over to him trustingly, saying, "Finally! I have been expecting you!"

Ariel could not understand anything whatsoever. He stood in the doorway, uncertain what to do.

"Sam has been complaining about a headache since morning," the woman said and held the child out to Ariel. "It's one trouble after another."

Ariel realized that she mistook him for a doctor. To untangle at least one misunderstanding, he said, "Forgive me, Madam, but I am not a doctor."

The woman's face blanched, she clutched the child to her, staggered back and asked fearfully, "Who are you? How did you get in? Are you from them? From these terrible people trying to get my son?" She paused, looking between Ariel and the little boy with the eyes filled with alarm.

No, Ariel was definitely not suited for this. The best he could do was turn, run into the next room, and fly out of the window, allowing the poor woman to think that she hallucinated. But Ariel realized that he was deceived into some foul crime, and he wanted to uncover the truth.

"Forgive me, Madam, do not be afraid. I will explain everything. Apparently, there has been some sort of misunderstanding."

"George!" the woman shouted, shaking all over.

Her anxiety transferred to the boy, and he started crying again.

There was a sound of quick footsteps, and a middle-aged man entered the room. At the sight of Ariel, he went as pale as his wife and stepped between them, as if shielding her. He asked sternly, almost rudely, "Who are you? What do you want?" He then looked closer at Ariel's face and exclaimed with sincere surprise, "Mister Binoy?"

"And what is your name, sir?"

"Warrender. What can I do for you?"

"Warrender?" Ariel exclaimed, equally surprised. They looked at each other in confusion for some time. Then Ariel, finally convinced that he had been deceived, decided to honestly tell everything to Sam's parents.

"I must speak with you, sir."

In Warrender's study, Ariel told them how he was drawn into the matter, omitting only his ability to fly.

"They wanted to use my exceptional agility. I came in from the window of the nearby apartment, along the ledge. I am very glad that I did not become a tool of these terrible people," Ariel concluded.

Warrender shook his head and said, "I believe you, Mister Binoy. You were deceived and acted out of generosity and kindness. Forgive me, but despite your athletic genius, you are clearly a very inexperienced young man and unfamiliar with our country. Although, to tell you the truth, such cunning approach could confuse anyone, even someone with more experience. I shudder to think! Had my wife not been with Sam because he hasn't been feeling well, the catastrophe would have been unavoidable. Our boy would have perished and our lives would have been ruined. These devious and ruthless people had hoped that, having participated in one of their crimes, willingly or unwillingly, you would have compromised yourself enough to give them power over you and make you their weapon. Of course, they could turn you in and have you executed at any time, blaming all their misdeeds on you alone. The police are in their pocket. It's terrible! Another one of their attempts had failed. But what will happen tomorrow?"

Mister Warrender, in turn, told Ariel about the nightmare he and his wife endured for an entire month. He showed the anonymous letters, demanding money.

"I have already paid out a lot, but the more I gave them, the more they demanded, threatening to kidnap the child. We moved here from our country home for safety. We hoped that all we had to do was watch the doors and not worry about the windows. I hired staff specifically to watch everyone who came in, but who can vouch that some of the servants are not the gangsters' accomplices? I think we have no other choice but to leave this country," he concluded sadly.

Ariel looked at his watch. It was almost midnight. He rose to leave.

"I believe you, Mister Binoy," Mister Warrender said. "You don't act like a criminal. You may leave the apartment safely, and no one will stop you. But I must warn you, you cannot just avoid these people. You have ruined their plans. Your life is in great danger. The best thing you can do is leave New York immediately, and get out of the country if you can."

"Thank you for your advice, Mister Warrender! That is exactly what I intend to do. You are right. Even a good deed in this country can turn into a terrible crime!"

Mister Warrender shook the hand of a man who almost took his son away to die a terrible death.

Having left Warrender's study, Ariel walked down the hallway, deep in thought.

So this was the price he had to pay for his ability to fly! Piers, the raja, the pastor, Chatfield, and the gangsters – they only wanted him as a weapon for their personal use. How could he find his own independent path and build a normal, honest life for himself?

The miraculous gift people covet in their dreams, had turned into a curse.

No, he had to escape this city and its coarse and cruel people.

What was he to do next?

His position was very precarious. What if Warrender and his wife changed their minds and decided to call the police after all? Besides, the gangsters and their accomplices might also be keeping an eye on the building. Ariel decided to leave through one of the hallway windows.

He flew across the city as fast as he could. Noticing a dark area in the park, he landed quickly and walked out into an alley.

Several people ran toward him, clearly having noticed the descent of some strange object.

"Did someone fall?" one of them asked.

"Not someone, but something," another one said. "Did you see anything, Mister?" he addressed Ariel.

"Yes, I saw something. Over there. I think it's beyond the fence, by the flower bed," Ariel replied, pointing off to the side.

As soon as they left, he ran on with a sigh of relief. It appeared everything was going to end well after all.

CHAPTER FORTY-FOUR. RETURN TO FRIENDS

"Why are you late? Where is your luggage? Why are you out of breath?" Jane showered her brother with questions.

"Are you ready, Jane? Let's go quickly. I'll tell you about it along the way. I almost got into a lot of trouble."

In the car on their way to the port, he told his sister a made up story about being nearly abducted by gangsters for ransom, and how common it was in America. He managed to get away by performing a giant leap. No, no, he didn't fly. This was no different than what he did at the circus. He told her how glad he was that she had already purchased the tickets.

"Now you see that I was right to insist on a speedy departure!" Jane lectured.

"I was thinking the same thing," Ariel replied sincerely.

Jane patted his hand patronizingly and said, "Always listen to me."

Ariel let out a sigh of relief only after the enormous ocean liner pulled away from the pier, and the band of water between him and the shore grew wider. He was glad that the gangsters couldn't fly.

Ariel stood on the deck, watching the city lights fade and disappear in the fog. This city was no less fascinating and terrifying than the distant Madras.

Their journey lasted many days. Every midnight, all ship's clocks were automatically moved an hour forward. From time to time, a powerful low-pitched siren shook the air, warning an oncoming ship. The passengers entertained themselves with movies and dancing, but Jane convinced Ariel not to leave his room. They were afraid that someone on the ship may have seen the "world champion – Binoy the Undefeated". He pretended to be sick and obligingly stayed in his room the entire time, feeling bored and watching the monotonous surface of the ocean through the porthole.

His only joy was the memory of his distant friends. He would not trade them for the world. He could not help but think about Lolita, Nizmat and little Sharad.

One time, when they were nearing London, Ariel couldn't stand it and told Jane about Lolita. Jane told her brother to describe the girl in detail, thought about it and said, "I wonder if she was that beggar that cried out when we found you by the roadside and took the sack off your head."

"Perhaps," Ariel replied. He did not know about this. Could Lolita really have been so close?

"And what do you think about this Lolita?"

"I... She is very poor, of course, although she is not a beggar. Millions of people in India live the same way. She is as beautiful as a dream. I love her very much and I shall never forget her."

"Don't tell me you intend to marry this gypsy filth?" Jane laughed with a dryly and condescendingly. "Just what we need! Splendid! Sir Aurelius Galton enters the lawful marriage with the Lady Lokita!"

"Her name is Lolita!" Ariel snapped.

Jane, considering the argument finished, said, "We need to order you some decent clothes, Aurelius. A tuxedo, a smoking jacket, a suit. In America, you dressed like an office clerk. My friend Barbara would laugh out loud if she saw you dressed like that."

Both during the trip and after they arrived, Jane refused to give her brother a moment's peace. It was as if he was suddenly assigned a stern governess, who constantly corrected him when he said or did something wrong. She made him smile and talk to people he found unpleasant, because it was good manners. She taught him to pay compliments. Ariel patiently tolerated this schooling, mentally calling it torture. Jane was particularly outraged by her brother's treatment of the servants.

"You talk to them as if they are your equals!" she exclaimed.

"Aren't they the same human beings as we are?" Ariel objected.

Jane lectured him endlessly about class inequality and about maintaining the air of cold politeness with the staff. With people of their own circle, however, he had to be exceptionally polite.

"But what if I can't stand that person?" Ariel said.

"No, you are impossible. You are utterly ill-mannered!" Jane cried out in frustration.

At onc point, Ariel, Jane and Dotaller traveled out of the city to look at the brick factories owned by the Galtons. Everything about them made Ariel depressed - squat barracks, clay soil, jagged queries, and water sloshing under the wooden platforms.

Jane did not notice any of it. After all, this mud was what their fortune was made of!

An old woman from the workers' village was crossing one of the bridges, fell, and could not get up.

Ariel ran to her and helped her up, soiling his kidskin gloves and his coat made by one of the best London tailors.

Ignoring Dotaller and the dismayed old woman, Jane scolded her brother. In her opinion, his actions were completely unwarranted. Ariel remained glumly silent and wiped his muddy hands with a handkerchief.

One week after their arrival to England, Ariel turned twenty-one and, therefore, came of age.

Jane anxiously prepared for this event, constantly telling Ariel that, on that day, he would be accepted into the highest levels of society.

Invitations were sent out to the best aristocratic families.

On the morning of Ariel's birthday, his guardians Boden and Heslon showed up.

What followed was an ugly scene between them and Jane. Jane asked the former guardians about the financial report, and feathers flew. Of course, neither she nor the guardians shouted or shook their fists at each other. On the contrary, the conversation was carried out in low voices, contributed by restrained gestures. But every word was filled with poison, and every glance was like an arrow. Essentially, this was the coarsest mercenary argument imaginable, complete with mutual accusations and insults.

Ariel was so depressed by the scene that he couldn't stand it and went to his room.

His nerves were on edge. He felt that the air was suffocating him. Despite chilly autumn weather, he opened a window, but only ended up letting clouds of fog and the smell of factory smoke into his room. Ariel slammed the window shut and paced around the room. He felt some kind of protest beginning to rise in his soul, a decision he felt he had to make.

The end of the day surpassed the limits of his patience.

When the guests assembled, Ariel thought he was witnessing some sort of a masquerade, a terrible parody of humankind. Everything was false here – false smiles, false words, false hair, teeth, and the ladies' complexion. Fresh faces were rare exceptions. There were women with unnaturally red hair, mottled skin and long teeth. The tuxedoed men were either rail-thin or suffocating with fat. Ariel had to shake hands with each one of them, smile his welcome, and say a few pleasant words. All this had to be done before Jane's piercing gaze, as she watched his every step and every word.

After dinner, the smug and imposing Lord Forbes started talking about India. He referred to the Indians as "those pigs" and "those crude animals worshipping a cow".

Ariel held back as long as he could, but finally blurted out, "Most of these simple, honest, hardworking people deserve more respect than those seated at this table, especially considering that you live at their expense!"

This was scandalous. Everyone went silent. Lord Forbes shook with rage and started crushing his unfinished cigar into the cigar box instead of an ashtray. Jane blanched, then summoned all of her self-control and tried to talk her way out of the embarrassing situation.

Once the guests were gone, however, she attacked Ariel with the full brunt of her anger! Forgetting good manners, she yelled that she refused to have a brother like that, that he wasn't an aristocrat but a pariah, that she would have to send him to an institution where they would make a real person out of him, or else they would have to part ways forever. Ariel would lose everything and would end up on the street, where he would find the kind of society he was so drawn to.

Much to her surprise and slight fear, Ariel spoke not one word of objection, remaining darkly calm.

Jane found this suspicious.

She pretended to feel bad and even apologized for her outburst.

"Of course, it is not your fault. One cannot go from the circus to a society assembly in a single leap. I am partly at fault myself. It was too soon to let you out into society. But you will understand…"

"I already understand. I understand everything," Ariel replied. "Don't worry, Jane. I won't cause you any more trouble. It's late. I am tired. Good night!" He went to his room, leaving his sister confused.

Ariel locked his door, paced the room for some time, then calmly packed some necessities and left the house with a modest suitcase.

The night was foggy. He could barely see beyond a few paces ahead. Ariel hired a cab and asked to be taken to the seaport.

Much to his joy, he found out that a large ocean liner traveling between London, Bombay, Colombo and Madras was leaving in an hour. He bought a third-class ticket – the thought of traveling in the company of people like Sir George Forbes, the Member of Parliament and the cause of the last argument with Jane, was intolerable.

In an hour, the enormous ship pushed away from the shore and headed off to distant India.

People on the pier watched as the dark indistinct mass made its way through the fog, sparkling with its portholes. At that early morning hour, the ship looked like some sort of a fantastic monster from someone's imagination. For some time, the lights flickered weakly, growing paler and more indistinct. Finally, they too vanished in the fog.

The ship taking Ariel away disappeared like a dream.

ABOUT THE AUTHOR

Alexander Romanovich Belyaev was born in 1884 in Smolensk, in the family of a Russian Orthodox minister. His sister Nina and brother Vasily both died young and tragically.

Following the wishes of his father, Alexander graduated the local seminary but decided not to become a minister. On the contrary, he graduated a passionate atheist. After the seminary he entered a law school in Yaroslavl. When his father died unexpectedly, Alexander had to find ways to make ends meet including tutoring, creating theater sets and playing violin in a circus orchestra.

Fortunately, his law studies did not go to waste. As soon as Belyaev graduated the law school, he established a private practice in his home town of Smolensk and soon acquired a reputation of a talented and shrewd attorney. He took advantage of the better income to travel, acquire a very respectable art collection and create a large library. Belyaev felt so secure, financially, that he got married and left his law practice to write full-time.

At the age of thirty-five Belyaev was faced with the most serious trial of his life. He became ill with Plevritis which, after an unsuccessful treatment attempt, developed into spinal tuberculosis and leg paralysis. His wife left him, unwilling to be tied to a sick man. Belyaev spent six years in bed, three of which – in a full-torso cast. Fortunately, the other two women in his life – his mother and his old nanny – refused to give up on him. They helped seek out specialists who could help him and took him away from the dismal climate of central Russia to Yalta – a famous Black Sea resort.

While at the hospital in Yalta, Belyaev started writing poetry. He also determined that, while he could not do much with his body, he had to do something with his mind. He read all he could find by Jules Verne, H.G. Wells and by the famous Russian scientist Tsiolkovsky. He studied languages, medicine, biology, history, and technical sciences.

No one had a clear idea how, but in 1922 Belyaev finally overcame his illness and returned to normal life and work. To cut the cost of living, Belyaev moved his family from the expensive Yalta to Moscow and took up law once again. At the same time, he put all the things he learned during the long years of his illness to use, by weaving them into fascinating adventure and science fiction plots. His works appeared more and more frequently in scientific magazines, quickly earning him the title of "Soviet Jules Verne".

After successfully publishing several full-length novels, he moved his family to St. Petersburg (then Leningrad) and once again became a full-time writer. Sadly, the cold damp climate had caused a relapse in Belyaev's health. Unwilling to jeopardize his family's finances by moving to yet another resort town, he compromised by moving them somewhat further south, where the cost of living was still reasonable – to Kiev.

The family didn't get to enjoy the better climes for long. In 1930 the writer's six-year old daughter died of meningitis, his second daughter contracted rickets, and his own illness once again grew worse.

The following years were full of ups and downs. There was the meeting with one of Belyaev's heroes – H.G. Wells n 1934. There was the parting of ways with the magazine *Around the World* after eleven years of collaboration. There was the controversial article *Cinderella* about the dismal state of science fiction at the time.

Shortly before the Great Patriotic War (June 22, 1941 – May 9, 1945), Alexander Romanovich went through yet another surgery and could not evacuate when the war began. The town of Pushkin, a St. Petersburg suburb, where Belyaev and his family lived, became occupied by the German troops. Belyaev died of hunger in January, 1942. A German general and four soldiers took his body away and buried it somewhere. It was highly irregular for the members of the German military to bury a dead Soviet citizen. When asked about it the general explained that he used to enjoy Belyaev's books as a boy, and considered it his duty to bury him properly.

The exact place of Belyaev's burial is unknown to this day. After the war, the Kazan cemetery of the town of Pushkin received a commemorative stele as the sign of remembrance and respect for the great author.

ABOUT THE TRANSLATOR

Maria K. is the pen name of Maria Igorevna Kuroshchepova – a writer, translator, and blogger of Russian-Ukrainian decent. Maria came to the United States in 1994 as an impressionable 19-year old exchange student. She received her Bachelors and Masters degrees in engineering from Rochester Institute of Technology (Rochester, NY).

Maria covers a wide range of topics from travel and fashion to politics and social issues. Her science fiction and fantasy works include Limited Time for Tomato Soup, The SHIELD, The Elemental Tales and others.

A non-fiction and science fiction writer in her own right, Maria is also a prolific translator of less-known works of Russian and Soviet literature into English. Her most prominent translations include her grandfather Vasily Kuznetsov's Siege of Leningrad journals titled The Ring of Nine, and Thais of Athens – a historic novel by Ivan Yefremov. Both works quickly made their way into the top 100 Kindle publications in their respective categories and continue attracting consistent interest and acclaim from readers.

END NOTES

[i] Dhoti – a man's garment that looks like wide pants or a skirt.
[ii] Zamindar – landlord.
[iii] Saniasi – saint.
[iv] Dada – brother.
[v] Anna – during the British colonial rule, a small coin valued at 1/16 of a rupee.
[vi] Zenan – a portion of the house reserved for women and inaccessible to visitors.
[vii] Cror equals one hundred lacks, one lack is a hundred thousand rupees.
[viii] Pronam – a greeting from an inferior to a superior.